WE'LL BE OKAY

KAYLA VILLANUEVA

DORRANCE PUBLISHING CO
EST. 1920
PITTSBURGH, PENNSYLVANIA 15238

Dorrance Publishing Co
585 Alpha Drive
Pittsburgh, PA 15238
Visit our website at *www.dorrancebookstore.com*

ISBN: 979-8-8860-4076-0
eISBN: 979-8-8860-4976-3

We finally made it to the boarding school at least. There is me and six of my friends; no adults are with any of us anymore. There is me (Miranda), Kevin, Justin, Miko, Allison, Victoria, and Alex. Allison and I are in "charge" of the group, Kevin and Alex are with me as hunters, Victoria is our nurse/cook, Miko and Justin are with Allison in gardening and lookouts. We started in the Bronx, and now we are in North Carolina… Oh, and I forgot to mention, we are in the zombie apocalypse.

*   *   *

I go to Allison's room and shake her. "Wake up. We need to get started. We are burning daylight."

"Okay, okay, I'm coming," she says. We head into the courtyard, where Justin and Miko just finished their lookout shift. Victoria is cooking, and Alex and Kevin are training. We stand on top of the tables.

"Guys!" I yell; everyone turns to face us. "Listen up. Today we decided to change it up a little. Miko, you will be coming with Kevin and I to the hunting grounds. Allison and I decided it's time to teach some of you other skills. Justin, you stay with Victoria, while, Alex, you go with Allison to the greenhouse right after breakfast," I finish. We hop off the table. I can tell Miko is nervous about it being her first time going hunting, but I'm sure it will be fine.

After breakfast, we set out. I have my gun in one hand and my dagger in the other as they follow close behind me. After a few minutes of not finding anything, Kevin spots a rabbit. Miko takes aim with her bow and arrow and hits the rabbit dead on. "Wow, nice shot." We give each other a high five and go collect dinner.

"Miranda…" Kevin hesitates. I try to face him, but before I can fully turn, I feel a gun barrel shoved into the back of my head and I instantly freeze. Out of the corner of my eye, I can see Kevin and Miko with guns to the back of their heads too. "Look, we don't want any trouble. Please," Kevin begs.

"We don't want to hurt you, kids. We just want your food," the man standing behind me says. I try to think of the best situations out of this mess. Either we try to fight back, but might be outmatched since Alex isn't here, or we let them have it and go. As I quickly try to go for my gun, I feel a hard kick in the back of my leg, and I fall. Now the gun is directly aimed at my forehead. "I'll shoot, kid," he says.

"Fine, take it," I say through clenched teeth; the three of them look like crackheads who just got out of rehab but are starting to relapse again. Once they are fully gone, I try to stand but my leg feels like glass that just shattered. "Fuck! Guys, I don't think I can get up." I wince.

That's when we start to hear that inhuman gurgling and smell the nauseating stench of these undead creatures coming closer; there are at least ten of them. "Guys, y'all have to move now," I say, trying to stand again but failing again miserably.

"I'm not leaving you here," Kevin says, throwing one of my arms over his shoulder and the other over Miko's. We get inside the school, and I still can barely use my leg.

"What the fuck happened to you guys?" Victoria asks as she rushes over to us. "Come bring her inside." She inspects my leg and bandages it up. "Miranda, seriously? Your leg is sprained pretty badly. I don't think you should be on it for at least two weeks and that is even risky." She sighs before walking out.

I've never been so pissed at myself; I showed weakness, hesitation, and fear, and I let down my guard for the smallest second that caused the biggest mistake. Now those assholes got away with our dinner for today. Something tells me that won't be the last time we see them. There is no way in hell I'm not going to walk, I *need* to. I go to stand up and immediately regret it when my leg gives out, like Bambi when he tried walking for the first time. I catch myself before falling and take a seat. I grab my leg and put my head down. Not being able to walk makes me feel like I'm letting down the group. I'm co-leader for god's sake! The person I'm letting down the most is Allison, and she needs someone there to help her. I don't want to leave all the responsibility on her. I try to sniffle my cry, but it isn't working, so I cave and let the tears fall down my face.

The first time I cried in six months.

Alex sees me. "Hey…I heard what happened. I'm sorry I wasn't out there with you guys."

"It's not your fault, Alex." He tries to help me stand but notices I can't even do that.

"You can hop on my back." He turns around and I jump on. We both laugh, and he carries me to the others. "I am now your human cab," he says, and I hold on tighter.

It's going to be a long two weeks. It's all fun and games with the whole back thing, but I still have a bad feeling. On top of beating myself up for a careless mistake but…those people, something horrible is coming, and it's not just the zombies.

*   *   *

It's been another week and not doing anything is a living hell. I know my leg is getting better because I can sorta limp. Victoria screams every time she sees me up, but she'll live. Sure, Allison comes into my room if she needs help making a decision, but I haven't been able to do much of anything physically, and it is killing me. "Hey, how are you feeling?" Allison walks in.

"I'm okay, how's everyone?" I say.

"Welllll, that's kind of what I wanted to talk to you about. Kevin and Alex went out yesterday; they said they heard a branch snap and felt like they were followed. They tried throwing anything off our trail but…I don't know," she says.

"Well, that means everyone just needs to—" I'm cut off by the sound of gunshots. Allison jumps up and pulls out her handgun. She motions for me to stay here and she runs off. There is no way I'm just going to sit here. I stand up and wince slightly in pain. When I finally reach outside, it looks like a scene out of a movie. It's those people from the woods, but this time they have more people. I see two of their guys shot dead. Justin and Alex are hiding behind a table. Victoria is hiding in bushes. Miko has been shot in the arm. Allison has a gun to her head, and Kevin is in a standoff with the guy who has her. I make my way over to Kevin and pull out my gun too. "What do you guys want!?" I yell.

The guy's grip tightens around Allison's neck. "Take a step further and I'll blow her brains out. It's pretty simple, kid, we want this school. We've been outside surviving for months! When we saw this place, we thought it would be perfect, and then found out it was run by kids! It couldn't have been a better set up," he finishes. There are five of us and five of them. I know we can take them on, we just have to be smart about it. I look over at Justin and Alex and give them a nod; they jump up and start shooting, and me and Kevin fire our shots to the guy. I hit his arm, and Kevin hits him right in the head.

Killing Him

It's been a little over a week; Miko can barely use her arm, but thankfully, it wasn't her shooting arm. My leg feels a lot better; I can't run or walk for too long but I'm able to move around at least; Kevin has barely said a word since the incident. It was hard for him to start killing zombies; he hated killing people in cold blood. He had to kill one of our best friends who was turning, and ever since then he swore he would try to never kill a human. We are all sitting in silence. "Hey, Kevin," Miko says, but there was no answer. "I'm sorry that you had to do that." Still no answer. "You saved Allison's life." He doesn't say a word.

I stand up. "Look you saved lives doing what you did. Stay quiet all you want, but we still have work to do whether you like it or not. We can't just sit on our asses and feel sorrowful for people who deserved to die," I say.

"They didn't deserve to die, and they were trying to survive like everyone else," he replied.

"You sound really stupid right now," I respond, causing him to stand and face me. "It is an us-or-them kind of situation. You kill when you have to." Justin quickly got in between us.

"Guys, arguing with each other isn't going to make it better," Justin intervened. "Miranda, go take a walk. Alex and Allison can go with you. Victoria, Miko and I will stay with you, Kevin," he says.

"Be back in like an hour! Dinner will be made by then!" Victoria says, and we walk off around the school. I don't like fighting with anyone in the group, but he just got me so mad that I couldn't help it. I'M in charge, not him; he needs to listen and respect my decision and actions.

After a few minutes of walking my leg started to cramp up. "Guys, I need a minute," I say. "Alex, I need my cab services." He turns around and I jump on. "Thank you."

"Miranda, you should apologize to Kevin. You know it wasn't easy for him, and you were a bit harsh,'" Allison says. I know she is right, it just sucks.

We are all we have left for each other, we shouldn't be arguing over stupid shit that isn't necessary.

We head back to the front of the school and eat dinner in silence. I know we are all used to silence, but this silence was way more awkward and uncomfortable than usual, and I don't like it. It's like you can feel and see the tension in the air.

"Look, I'm sorry for snapping at you, Kev. I know it was uncalled for. I apologize."

Justin nudges Kevin on the shoulder to speak. "I'm sorry too," he replies.

"Now that that is cleared, let's play a game!" Miko exclaims.

"Really, a game?" Alex asks.

"I mean, why not?" Justin adds.

"What game do we even play?" Victoria asks.

"Let's play Uno," Allison suggests. Everyone nods, and I get the cards.

We are in the middle of the second game, when Victoria plays a plus four. "Fuck you," Allison says. Everyone laughs, but Victoria seems pissed.

"It's just a game, no need to get bitchy," Victoria says.

"It was a joke. Damn, V, I didn't mean it," Allison says.

"Uhhh, guys, let's remember this is only a game," Miko tries to intervene.

"She needs to know how to take a joke," Allison replies.

"Well, fuck you. No I don't," Victoria snaps.

Victoria stands, and I stand before anything happens. "Both of you need to chill the hell out and remember it's a game. Victoria, sit…*now*," I say.

"You guys may be in charge, but you don't control me," she huffs. "And before I say something I regret, I'm going for a walk." She walks off out of the gate.

"Someone go after her. It's not safe at night," I say, and Alex goes off after her. Great, I'm leading a group of children who can't even play a game together. They tell me to be nice, and yet they almost have a full-blown fight as well. When the hell are these two going to be back? It is not safe to be out there alone this late, especially with no light or weapons.

"Maybe you should go for them? They don't have anything, and it's been a while," Justin suggested.

"Yeah, you're right." Miko nods. We all hear a high-pitch scream and jump up.

"Was that Victoria?" Kevin asks. I nod and feel a pit grow in my stomach and my forehead breaks out in a cold sweat.

"Kevin, you come with me, and Allison, you two stay here," I tell everyone as the three of us take off running into the night.

We take off into the woods, trying to follow the scream. We find Alex and Victoria cornered by the zombies that are approaching them on all sides.

"I don't know what we should do," I say.

"I don't think we can save both of them…Miranda, it's us or them," Kevin replies. There are at least twenty-five zombies surrounding them, and I can see more coming. We don't have enough bullets or weapons for all of them.

"No! We are not leaving anyone behind," Allison says.

"Whatever we do, we have to move fast or we are all dead," I say quickly. I think Kevin is right on this one, I don't see how it is possible to save both of them, but that doesn't mean I'm not going to try. "I say we run in and just go for it," I suggest.

"This is why I am co-leader with you, Miranda," Allison replies.

"How about the three of us start shooting. Each clip holds eight or ten rounds, right? We just have to be fast," she asks.

"Okay…let's do it," I say. "Alex, Victoria, RUN!" They duck and weave, trying to run away from the zombies and bullets. We all keep shooting while running back to the school. Allison, Kevin, and I get split up, but I just keep running and shooting. I can't stop now. I make it back to the school, panting. I look around and see everyone crowded around and crying. "Guys, what's wrong?" I ask, before going to see why they are crying. It's Kevin, he was lying on the ground, a small pool of blood leaking from a huge tear in his shirt…. He was bitten.

"There is nothing I can do for a bite," Victoria sadly says.

"We are going to have to kill him," Justin adds.

"No!" Miko and Allison shout at the same time.

"No! Isn't there something we can do?" I frantically asked as I crouch closer. I can see his eyes darkening like death, blood starts dripping from his mouth, you can see a fever skyrocketing as sweat drips from his forehead and body. But I can also see him fighting like hell to stay with us. I know what I have to do. I know after this, things won't be normal, but we will still be together. I *have* to do it. With tears in my eyes, I stand up and hold the gun out. *The first time I have ever trembled and hesitated with a gun.*

"Miranda…Do what you have to do…I'll be okay."

Bang.

Since then, I have never been the same…

*   *   *

Two months…It has been two fucking months since Kevin's death, and honestly the tension is so thick with the group you can cut it with a knife. We barely speak to each other, and I haven't slept a full night since; the guilt is eating me up inside. I replay that situation and those last words he said to me, *I'll be okay.* Is this just a sign that the inevitable is happening? I would rather it had been me than him; there isn't a day, hour, or minute that goes by that I don't think about how I failed the group; how I failed him. He was the one I could go to if I ever got too stressed. Now the stress just adds up. "Miranda…. MIRANDAAAA," Allison says. I somehow snap back into reality, if that's what you wanna call this. "Did you hear what I just told you?"

"No. I'm sorry," I say

"I said it's time to go out and you are taking Justin with you and Alex," she says.

"Okay." I stand up and grab my gun. As soon as I grip the gun, I hear the bang coming from it. I jump, and the gun almost drops. I quickly snatch it in mid-air and hold it tighter. This gun is what holds our world together today, in life or death, and its decisions are still in my hands. I go outside and all eyes are on me; I hate that feeling. It's like when a rumor in school about you and everyone sucks at hiding it. "Guys, come on. Let's go," I say and we walk off. It seems to be peacefully quiet in the forest today; it's sunny with not a cloud in the sky. It is airy but not cold, and it gives you time to get lost, in a good way. The perfect place you would go to if you ever felt sad, mad, or overwhelmed back in the day.

"Miranda, look!" Justin shouts. It was an abandoned house, and it looked like there was a clear pathway to it.

"What do we have to lose?" I ask as we all pull out our guns and go in.

"Alex, you check upstairs; Justin, downstairs with me, and I'll check the kitchen."

*   *   *

The search was a HUGE win for us today. We raided an abandoned house and found a bunch of canned food that will last us a while at least. I sit alone while I eat dinner again, because it's really hard to look in anyone's eyes after what happened. "Hey," Alex says and sits down next to me.

"Hey…." I say.

"Look, I know it's hard for you right now. Hell, it's hard for us all. Just know that we are here for you. You're not alone anymore," he says, and he is right.

In the very beginning of this whole thing I was with my "real family" for about four months. I remember us trying to celebrate my brother turning thirteen even though we had no idea if the days were right. It's been so long since that time, it didn't even feel like a month ago, but at the same time it felt like years. Staying with them was horrible. I saw my mom suffer in silence due to all her medical problems, my brother not know what to do or how to do it, my dad never listening to anything I had to say, and my sister who was too afraid to do anything. Until, one day, we all went out and got attack by way more zombies than I ever imaged, and I was able to make it out of the attack…. *Only me.* I had to watch as my family died in front of my eyes because I was too scared to move. My dad didn't make a sound; he knew it was all over for him, so he gave up, but I had to hear the deaf-defying, scared screams of my siblings, the heartbroken and trembling cries of my mom. A week later, I ran into Allison and Miko while they were trying to break into a store. I was scouting for people to stay with, so, when I first saw them, I didn't believe it was them. We had roughly started junior year this same year, it was like our fourth, fifth month? I can't remember, so when I saw them, I didn't run to them. I called out for them, and they looked terrified yet relieved. We made it as a three-person group for a little over three weeks, but it wasn't easy. We were staying in a little abandoned house, and we didn't do any hunting; instead, we went scouting. Well, I went. I didn't want them to risk their lives. I was coming back from scouting, when I saw Kevin on the side of the road.

At first, I thought he was dead, so I walked away, but he came up to me and we went back together. We were just the four of us for over a month, but a group had "taken us in," and one of the lead soldiers there was Alex. We only lasted a week there until Alex got kicked out, and we left with him. This time I was positive the group was done because we had been together for five months, and we had a working car. It was surprising to all of us that we were still alive, and then Allison spotted Victoria and Justin a month later as they were trying to fight off a zombie. I guess it was only a matter of time before things fell apart. You piece together a group of teenagers, and a world of the dead, bad things are bound to happen and once they do… They never stop. Rethinking those memories made my heart ache and my head spin.

"Miranda? Miranda!" is all I heard before I blacked out. I woke up the next day with a pounding headache, and I mean, I never had a hangover, but this feels like what it would be. "Thank god. How are you feeling?" Miko asks while entering the room.

"I'm okay. What the hell happened?" I ask.

"Victoria says your fainting was probably caused by over-emotional emotions. I'm sure the group will be happy to know you're okay," she says.

"Yeah…" I don't even know what to say.

"What's wrong?" she asked.

"Nothing. Don't worry," I stand up. "I'm okay." I know I'm not okay, and she knows too. She gives me the "I-know-you're-lying" look, but I walk past her.

Three more days go by, and things go on as usual. I still eat alone, and I've grown accustomed to it. "You wanna play a game?" Allison says.

"Really? The last time we played a game it didn't go so well…." I say.

"Come on, have some hope," Allison says, pulling out a deck of regular cards.

"Fine, nobody better get into a fucking argument or I swear to god—" I get cut off by a stern look from Allison.

"I'm sorry," I say, while looking down and fiddling with my fingers.

Everyone joins the table. "So what game we are playing?" Justin asks.

"Let's play Go Fish!" Miko yells over excitedly, and we all just shrug. Allison deals out everyone's cards and we start playing.

"Got any threes?" I ask, and everyone shakes their heads. "Ahhhhhhh."

We all laugh. It felt good to finally laugh again as a group; it was nice to smile a real smile and be genuine, and it was nice to sit down and have a normal night and talk. They are my home. They are my family.

After a couple rounds it was time to hit the hay, but I had watch duty with Allison and then with Miko, so I had a longggg night ahead. Since it has been hard for me to sleep, I usually work double shifts with whoever goes for the nights. Allison and I are sitting just watching ahead, "Hey, can I ask you something?" she asks.

"Sure," I say.

"Do you think this apocalypse will ever end?" she asked.

"Honestly, I would hope so, but as realistic as I can think, no, I don't think so, because the numbers are growing with the zombies instead of dying out. Instead, we humans are dying out, and it's not like we aren't going to keep dying, dying is inevitable," I say.

She looks out into the distance "I know you're right, but it's just nice to think about a possible different life." She sighs and rests her head on my shoulder. I put my head on top of hers, and for some reason my heart started to race and stomach does flips; this can't be good.

Allison ended up falling asleep, and usually I would wake her up, but tonight I let her sleep; she deserved it. Miko comes up for her time. "Isn't it my turn?" she asks, and I nod. I get Allison to get on my back and I carry her down and to her room. I place her down in her bed, a small smile falls on my lips.

"Goodnight," I whisper and leave the room. I make my way up to the lookout post and Miko was sitting there.

"Took you long enough." We laugh, and I take a seat with her.

"Well, I'm here now and that is all that matters," I say.

"True," she replies.

"Hey, do you think the apocalypse will be over one day?" I ask.

"I would only hope," she responds. "But how have you been feeling? I know Victoria and Justin are kind of being rude lately." She's right. The more and more I try to speak to everyone, they either cut me off, shut me down, or ignore me. I even noticed Alex doing it.

"I try not to put too much effort into it. If I do, I will go even more insane," I reply. To be honest, I just don't want to cause problems within the group. Miko and I spent the rest of the night making horrible jokes and laughing. *I'm glad she's on my side.*

*   *   *

Something is seriously up with Alex, Victoria, and Justin, and it's really upsetting me. I don't know what I did wrong. I thought it would be over. I never felt like I belonged anywhere, but they are the best people that ever happened to me and the fact that some of them are blowing me off is really messing with my heart. Right now, I'm sitting in my room alone, just thinking and throwing a ball at my wall. I have some pictures that my brother and I drew up on my wall. I had some real pictures, but I tore them down, we all did. We wanted to forget and start over.

"We thought we heard something," Allison says, and she and Miko enter. They have been getting a lot closer lately, and even though my mind tells me it's fine, I can't help not liking it. I mean, we are family and stuff, but they have been spending a lot more alone time and sharing more inside jokes. I'm sure it's nothing, I'm probably having abandonment issues right now.

"Yep, the loner." I laugh.

"Why don't you tell others how you feel?" Miko asks. She makes a good point. I mean I am in charge of these people, and without me, *and Allison of course*, we would be nowhere.

"I—" I'm cut off again! *I just love getting cut off…*

"You know what, I'll tell them," Allison says, and Miko and I follow her out. She jumps on the table to catch everyone's attention. "Listen up!" she yells.

I see Victoria roll her eyes. "What now? I thought today was our day off!"

"Just shut up and listen for once," Allison yells.

"I don't know why you guys are doing this, but stop ignoring Miranda. Did you guys forget that without her we would have all been dead a very long time ago? Did you guys forget that she is in charge here with me? I don't know why you are upset, but you guys have to realize that it's stupid and probably not needed. We are a family, and right now you guys are not acting like one," she says sternly, and everyone except Miko looks even more annoyed than when she started to speak.

Victoria then chimes in, "Well, maybe if she wasn't careless, our WHOLE family would still be here."

"Are you fucking kidding me!" I yell and try to go and hit her, but Miko pulls me back. "Do you remember we ran out there to save you!" I yelled angrily. I swear to god, I wanna bash this girl's fucking head in.

"You lost him in the mix of things, so what kind of leader are you?" she counters coldly.

"How could you say something like that? It was your damn attitude that made us go out there! It's not my fault you can't take a damn joke!" I struggle, trying to free myself out of Miko's grip. When the hell did this girl get so strong?

"Victoria! How dare you!" Allison yells in shock and jumps down from the table. "She saved your fucking life!" she said louder as she stepped to her.

"Please, she didn't do shit except for almost putting our whole group in danger," Victoria stated.

"But she did it for you," Miko said, at least she has her head on straight.

"Victoria is right, guys," Justin said. "How you guys say it went down sounds very careless and unsafe. If you guys would have had a real plan, maybe Kev would still be here," he says.

"Shut the fuck up. You shouldn't even be speaking. You didn't even wanna help us save her!" I shout.

"You weren't even there, Justin. If you're gonna blame her, then you have to blame me. I'm the one who told her we should save the both of you and not leave anyone behind," Allison says. She turns and faces me. "You should blame me. I blame me." She turns to Alex. "Alex, come on. You know this isn't right," she adds, but he holds his hands up.

"I don't wanna get involved in this." I glare at him.

"I'm sorry," he says and backs up.

"I thought I could at least trust you, Alex…after everything," I say, and he doesn't look at me. I know he is replaying those memories in his head, but, honestly, to hell with him too right now.

"Kevin died because of you," Victoria says, and she points right at me. The accusation and thoughts fill my head again and I think of all the possibilities…. She's right isn't she? I should have watched and kept a closer eye on my group. Should have seen the pieces start to crack and the foundation shaking. I don't feel like a real leader. I probably don't deserve to have this position. I could have done more, I know I could have, but I didn't, and that's a shame on me...

"Don't listen to her." Allison comes to comfort me. When her back is turned, I can see Victoria charging at her.

"Allison, look out!" Miko shouts, and Allison turns around and stabs Victoria in her stomach with her knife. When she pulls the knife out, at first she looks taken aback, but suddenly an evil glint flashes in her eyes that I have never seen before, and she stabs Victoria again, in the chest, then in the stomach, and again in the chest. You can hear the sound of each stab tear through Victoria's clothes, then skin and go inside Victoria. Each time Allison pulls the knife out, blood splatters. Victoria tries to beg Allison to stop, but she won't; instead, she puts the knife to her throat and starts cutting slowly, as if she wanted to see all the blood drain from Victoria's face and body. We see Victoria's eyes roll in the back of her head, and she starts coughing up blood.

"Allison, stop!" Justin yells while trying to pull Allison off Victoria, but Allison stabs him in his chest and twists her knife. "I… Fuck, Alli…" Justin collapses. Seeing Justin fall seems to make her snap back into reality, and she stands up, both her hands drowned in blood, her face smeared in it. She looked like one of the zombies; I've never seen her eyes just as soulless.

We all are just taken aback, and I make the first move. I push her against the wall and hold my arm to her neck. "I'm sorry, Miranda. I'm so sorry," she repeats. I have never seen Allison that way before. She has never lashed out this bad, not even when we were trying to kill the zombies, and hell, I haven't seen her this vulnerable since our high school days. She starts to cry, and my soft side kicks in and I hug her.

"I know you are." I let her cry on my shoulder for a little while but push her away slightly to take a look at our sister's and brother's bodies, *dead*.

We've lost three people in less than three months, and it seems like just yesterday when we were driving to the school. Victoria, she wasn't perfect and had a bitchy attitude, but she tried at least. She always wanted to help around the school and everything to be perfect. Justin, he was quiet yet persistent, and he always had a strategy and always thought of thousands of solutions. He almost never said no depending on the consequences; he was always hands-on for everything. I'm gonna miss them so much. This family is all I have left, and they are disintegrating so fast I can't even keep up with it. My heart starts aching so bad the more I stare at the bodies. We all gathered around them except Allison, she ran into her room. I let her be. I know she probably needs a minute after what just happened. I put my head down and cried. I hate fucking crying so much and I haven't cried so much in so long. I can't handle so many losses; I know we won't be the same. I deal with killing strangers and zombies, but the more I see a loved one either go or die, I lose a part of myself with them. I bent down and looked at them closer. Justin's eyes were still open, and the knife was still in his chest. I carefully remove the knife and chuck it as far as I can over the wall of the school, then I slowly close his eyes with my hand. "I love you, guys. I'm so sorry this happened." I stood up, pushed past Miko and Alex, and walked away.

This group is falling apart...

Well, it's been a while since Justin and Victoria died and Allison is now the one not talking to us. I've been hanging out with Alex, but he has been getting really touchy and it is kind of getting on my nerves. I hope he isn't getting the wrong idea because of what happened before this apocalypse ever happened. It was a one-time thing, he needs to move on. Allison only talks to Miko from time to time; she won't even talk to me when we need to make a decision; she either just nods or shakes her head. It really hurts to see her only talk to Miko and not me. I thought we told each other everything. Miko, I notice she has been trying to spend more time with Alex as well; whenever we need lookouts she volunteers if I tell him to do it. The height difference makes it amusing, though. I've been doing a lot of practice day in and day out, just to keep my mind off of everything and everyone.

I try to keep my mind off the fact that everyone in this group is finally starting to realize we are probably the only survivors we will meet, and we are teenagers, after all; hormones/experiments and just basic attractions start kicking in. I don't know if most of them are just petty crushes/lust or if some emotions are genuine, but that's for each of us to figure out. I guess it was bound to happen; the closer and more time you spend with one person or a group, no matter what feelings I guess are bound to emerge. If I think too much into it, I'll end up thinking about who I like and who I don't want to. I want to suppress those thoughts. I won't ruin a friendship over a stupid little crush. I mean, sure, *she is really, really pretty, smart, skillful, thoughtful—* SHUT UP! I punched the bag harder. Stop it, Miranda!

"Miranda, come here!" Miko yells. I go to her and see Allison packing the very few things she has. "Help me tell her to stop. She wants to leave us," Miko says.

"Its better for you all if I leave," Allison says.

"No, Allison, stop," I say, trying to grab the bag out of her hand, but she yanks it back. "Please, we need you here," I say, but she still isn't listening. "Please, Allison, think about this," I basically beg.

She sighs and puts her bag down. "Fine," she mumbles.

"Yay!" Miko yells. I just smile and don't say anything.

"Come with me." I grab both their hands and drag them out. I'm not gonna let history repeat itself with the awkwardness. "You sit here and you here." I place both of them across from each other. "Alex, come over here right now!" I yell. Alex sits with Miko, and I take a seat next to Allison.

"What are we doing?" Alex asked.

"We are going to have a heart-to-heart," I say.

"Uhh, what does that mean?" Miko asked.

"Why?" Allison finally says something.

"It's where we just talk, ask each other ANY questions, and because I say so," I answer. "Now I will go first. Alex, why didn't you want to get involved?" I ask.

He sighed, "I didn't want to get involved because I try to have no bias towards any of you, and if I tried to play fair for everyone, I feel like I would have just did more damage than good...."

I just nod. If he got involved defending either side, I guess it would have just added fuel to the fire. "Now, Alex, you can ask anyone here a question."

"Okay, Miko, what was your first time killing a zombie like?"

"Well, it was nerve racking, I was all alone, and I had a handgun but never used it before. I closed my eyes and just shot and got really lucky to have shot it in the head." We all laughed a little. Miko points to me. "Miranda, what really happened between you and Alex before? You guys look like good friends but sometimes look like exes," she asked. I knew this question would pop up; even in a dying apocalyptic situation people still want to know the gossip.

"Well..." I trail off. "I told you guys who he is already. Him and I were really close. We went on a couple dates, we never really made anything official. No, we didn't kiss or hookup." I glared at Alex.

"Even though I wanted to," Alex says, and I kick him under the table. "Ow, fuck, sorry." He grabs his knee.

"My turn. Miko, would you ever date Alex?" I ask, and she shifts uncomfortably.

"I mean, uh…" She blushed heavily and moved away from him slightly. "Yeah, I would." She looked down, and he just smiled.

"Best question asked ever." Allison laughs and high-fives me.

"Fine, if you guys are gonna tease me, then, Miranda and Allison, would you guys ever date each other?" she asked. We both go silent and look away from each other.

"I think it's time to stop with the question…" Allison trails off.

"Yes," I answer. Everyone looks at me, and my heart starts to beat really fast like I'm about to have a panic attack. "I…I'm so…sorry I…g-gotta go." I run into my room and sit in the corner taking deep breaths

I hear three soft knocks on my door, and before I can say anything, I hear, "It's me. Please let me come in," Allison whispers.

"C-come in. Door…isn-isn't locked," I stutter, and she comes in and sits next to me. At first it's silent, since I'm trying to focus on my breathing. This silence is so awkward. Why do we still even have feelings in the apocalypse? Why couldn't they go extinct like McDonald's or technology?

"How are you feeling?" she asks, and I just shrug.

"I mean how would you feel if you just admitted something like that?" I question and raise my eyebrows, and she just laughs a little.

"Touché. Hey, do you remember the time you and I got detention for skipping class?" he lightens up.

"It wasn't my fault we didn't study for the test! We were too busy living life!" I explain and we laugh. "You remember how we meet?" I ask.

"How can I forget, we were both awkwardly sitting by ourselves in class and you came up to me and asked for the answers," she answered. I hated math class. I saw her doing the work, and she looked like she knew what she was doing, so I asked, and sure enough, she did.

"Ever since that day, a beautiful friendship was formed," I exaggerate. "And now look at us." I sigh. She doesn't say anything at first; instead, she takes my hand and interlaces our fingers. "We are fighting for our lives every day, our family is dying, and we struggle to keep going. I know I do. It's been getting so much harder to get out of bed, to just give up and not come back, to end it all right here." I start to tear up but quickly wipe the tears away.

"I know how you feel. After what happened to Kev, I thought it was only a matter of time before we stopped talking to each other or go our separate ways. Then what I did to Victoria and Justin… I wanted to just end all the guilt I had right there and turn the knife to myself." She wipes her tears too. "But you stopped me, Miranda. You helped me stay and you try so hard to keep the peace in this place that it must be exhausting. I try to help, but I feel like things are out of my hands." She doesn't look up.

"Allison, if it wasn't for your calls, we would all be dead," I say. "You help more than you think," I finish. Neither of us says anything for a while; we just sit in silence. I finally got the courage to speak up. "You're one of the closest people I've ever known. You're one of the most important people left for me, Allison," I say, squeezing her hand sightly

"Shhhh," she says with a sly smile.

"I'm glad you feel the same," I joke, and she sighs out and rests her head on my shoulder.

"I don't ever want to lose you, Miranda," she says weakly. I put my head on hers and run my thumb on the back of her knuckles for reassurance. After a few seconds, I can feel myself starting to fall asleep, so I just let myself drift to sleep.

*   *   *

It's been a week since Allison and I had that talk and things are actually starting to look up in this grey world. Besides us just deciding to go with the flow, Alex and Miko are now apparently boyfriend and girlfriend. I'm so glad the group is at peace for now. We had our ups and downs, but I'm glad right now we are comfortable. I'm at the lookout spot right now, and I'm tracing the sun set. I used to draw a lot before this, and I try to keep up with it from time to time. I do still have trouble sleeping, but it's been getting a little better…at least I think. "Hey." Miko climbs up and sits next to me, and I cover my drawing.

"Hey, why are you here?" I ask.

"What? You don't want me here?" she teases. "What's that?" She points to the paper.

"Nothing important, it's stupid," I say. She grabs the picture from my hand and gets a better look. "Hey! That's mine." I snatch it back.

"It's really good. I didn't know you draw," she says.

"I did." *Back in the better days*, I think.

"I thought I heard you too up there! Come down! Breakfast is done!" Allison yells. Miko goes down and sits with Alex, and I stay put. "Miranda! You too!" she yells again.

"No!" I laugh. It's fun to piss her off...sometimes.

"Don't make me come up there!"

"Come! Be a lot more fun up here!" I tease and look down, seeing her cheeks burn red. "I'm coming!" I laugh as I climb down and hug her. "That better, boss?" I joke. We sit next to Alex and Miko and eat.

"Isn't it crazy?" Alex speaks up.

"What is crazy, babe?" Miko asked.

"That we are still pushing. Let me explain. We all started on our own, found each other, some of us died, and now the ones who are left are getting stronger every day and still pushing forward." We all just stared at him. "All I want to say is I'm thankful you guys are here with me, and I'm proud of how all of us became," he finishes, and we all raise our glasses.

"On that nice note. Let's talk chores." They all groan. "I know, but we all need to go out this time. Allison and I were thinking, and it's not safe for one of us to stay here while the others go out," I say, and Miko and Alex look hesitant. "I uhh…" I trail off.

Allison grabs my hand. "We are all going out after breakfast, got it?" she says sternly.

After breakfast we set out to go hunting, Miko and Alex are in front of us, and Alex has his arm around Miko. Allison and I are holding hands; Alex was right about this being very crazy, but I don't care. We are heading to the river to go fishing for dinner. Fishing is fun, so I'm happy about it. "We are here," Alex says and grabs the spears we hide. "This is so much fun." Alex hands them out and immediately gets to work on his side. I stab a fish dead on and put it into the bucket, and I can see Alex doing the same thing.

"Is this how you felt when you stabbed Victoria?" I joke to Allison, and she pushes me. I slip off one of the wet rocks, and before I fall, I jump into the river, my pants up to my knees getting wet. We all burst out laughing. I'm glad we are trying to make the best out of the worst situation.

A few minutes later I'm taking a break and so does Alex, because we have caught four each, and Allison only caught one, and Miko hasn't caught any. "I'm gonna go help Miko." Alex gets up and goes to teach Miko how to properly hold and use the spear. *The girl uses a bow and arrow but can't use a spear, how ironic*, I think. I wish we could go for a swim, or just do things for fun. It's like, now the only fun you can have is when you celebrate a win with getting food, supplies, or whatever. I just wish we could actually enjoy being teenagers, do all the things the movies and parents told us about. Like going to parties, pulling pranks on teachers, going to college, and just following our dreams.... Now we are following survival instincts.

I see Allison struggling and almost falling. "Don't fall," I say, and she just rolls her eyes. "It's freezing!" I laugh.

"Yeah, I know," she says. "I don't want to do anymore." She throws the spear down and sits next to me. "At least we have some food for tonight," she says and plays with my fingers.

"Yeah, awwww, look." I point at Alex and Miko holding the spear together and smiling. "They are adorable," I say, and she nods.

"We should start heading back." She stands up and grabs the buckets. "Let's go, guys!" she yells. Alex hides the spears again and grabs his bucket. We walk back to the school in a comfortable silence. The group seems to be getting stronger every day. Yes, we aren't perfect at all. No, we will never be the same, but we can learn to live. When we get back to the school, we notice a guy on his knees with his back to us.

Alex and I draw our guns. "Who the fuck are you?" I question, and he stands up.

"Put your hands up and turn around slowly," Alex says sternly. The guy slowly turns around, and Miko, Allison, and I freeze. I drop my gun, Miko just stays put, and Allison drops the bucket of fish.

"Jordan..." Miko and I say. No one says anything at all; we are too shocked to speak. Jordan was our friend back in high school, and when this whole thing broke out, we thought he was dead. We actually tried looking for him. We thought he would be with Victoria and Justin. Jordan and Allison use to date for a little while back in junior year, but it didn't exactly work out because they were always arguing over really stupid shit like after school. They didn't talk for months, before Allison and him could start talking again this happened.

"Who the fuck is this guy!" Alex says. I put my hand on his gun barrel and lower it "But…"

"No," I say sternly. "Speak. Are you bitten?" I ask, and he doesn't answer. His eyes are locked with Allison, who still hasn't moved since we started doing anything. I go up to him and snap my fingers in front of his eyes. "I asked you if you were bitten," I say.

"Oh, uh, no, I'm not. I got attacked by some people a while away." He lifts his pants leg and we see a huge gash in his cafe.

"Shit, uhh,…Miko, go take Jordan into the nursing room and see if you can clean and stitch up the gash," I tell her, and they go into the building, while Alex has a mean mug on his face and Allison looks lost on what to say. "Allison…you okay?" I ask.

"He needs to leave," she says angrily.

"Can someone please explain who the hell he is?" Alex asks.

"That is Jordan; we went to school together before this happened," I say

"Annnnd?" He waves his hand for me to continue.

"Also, Allison and him used to go out, and it didn't end the best way," I explain.

"He was an asshole," she spits out. "He never listened and made the dumbest comments just to trigger me on purpose so he could laugh and make jokes." She picks up the bucket and puts it on the table. "Once his leg is better he needs to leave."

"Maybe it could be good for us. We don't have much firepower or hands since the others passed. Maybe he could help, even if it is just a lookout." Alex suggested.

"You know, he makes a good point," I tell her.

"I mean I'm not saying he could stay forever. If he is bad in your book, then he is bad in mine. He can be a liability," Alex says.

"Ugh! You guys are ridiculous." She stomps her foot and walks away. Well, this is just what we need, to make the group a lot worse. Everyone is still very on edge. Yes, we are getting better, but three of our family members just died at the hands of the two coleaders who were supposed to keep them safe. Every now and then, when I walk past Allison's room, I think I can hear her crying. I went in the first couple of times and spent the night trying to make her feel better, and sometimes it worked. Other times she faced her back to me and wouldn't talk at all. I stopped going in after the third time she did that, figuring I'm only making things worse. I don't like Jordan at all, but Alex is right about him being a good addition to the group for now, since we are such short-handed. We just have to keep him at arms distance and keep a lookout on his behavior. I better go check on her...in like five minutes.

"Alex, is your girl any easier than her?" I ask, and he laughs.

"Miko is a lot easier to handle. In a good way, of course." He cracks a sly smile.

"Alex and Miko sitting in a—" He covers my mouth, and I bite his hand and he pulls away.

"Ow!" He shakes his hand out and it's my turn to laugh.

"I'm gonna go check on her," I tell him and run off into the school and go to her room. I knock on the door as I enter. "Heyyy…" I trail off.

"Go. Away." She turns away from me and folds her arms.

"Come on, don't be like that," I say, and she doesn't say anything and doesn't look at me still. "Allisonnn," I drag and put my chin on her shoulder. "Please talk to me," I ask.

"No." She shrugs me off and takes a step forward away from me. "I'm mad at you." She turns to face me. "We"—she gestures between the both of us—"and us in general were just starting to get better. I don't want him to mess it up, make things awkward, and drive us even more apart. I don't want wedges drawn, and I know Alex already doesn't like him. I just don't need the extra tension…." she trails off, and I grab her shoulders. I can tell she wants to go off, but her eyes shift into a sad puppy eyes. "I don't want him here." She hugs me tightly and puts her head on my shoulder, and I hug back and rub her back smoothly.

"I know you don't. If he stays, I'll personally keep an eye on him and make sure he doesn't bother you, okay?" I suggest, and she just nods and sniffles.

Miko comes in. "Oh, am I interrupting?" she asks. I pull away from Allison and face her.

"No," we say at the same time. I look over and see a slight blush on Allison's face.

"Okayyy, he looks fine, and he can walk. I don't suggest he run or be on it that much. It looks like he might have slashed it on a branch running away or someone came at him hard and he fought them off. And we should probably wait to talk to him, he is kind of out of it," she says, and we just nod.

How much worse can this get…

It's been four days and Jordan is finally able to communicate, so now it is time to get serious. I walk into the old nurse's office "We need to talk," I say while standing in the doorway.

"I know, I'll leave now," he tells me, sitting up.

"No, you can stay. But only as a pair of extra hands. You don't have a say in decisions, you play nice with everyone, and you make sure you don't upset Allison, or I will personally kill you with my bare hands," I say sternly, and he stares at me, stunned for a second, then just nods. "Good." I walk straight outside. "He is cool with staying here," I tell everyone. They roll their eyes and I hear Alex whisper something to Miko, and she nods. "Anyway, he is gonna stay, but the moment tension, awkwardness, or anything weird happens, he leaves," I say, but Allison still walks away. She will come around hopefully, I don't like it when she is mad at me.

"Are you gonna go check on her?" Miko asked.

I sigh and look in the direction she walked off to. "No, it's better if I leave her alone for a little bit," I say. "I'm gonna go up to the lookout post for a little while, and uh, I'll be down… Later." I leave them and sit in my spot. Why do we focus on all this petty shit? Like, we are dying, and instead of working, we are arguing. We try so hard to act like adults and handle situations maturely, but at the end of the day we are teens, we have hormones and inexperience. We are just trying to make it out alive without any dumb decisions, yet we have no idea what we are doing and still fall on our faces because we are human! We are young and have no idea what we are doing and just scraping by the skin of our teeth every day, and it is draining. I wish I brought my pencil and paper. I left it in Allison's room. I started this drawing that I want to work on…. Guess it has to wait. I remember the "old days"—*God, I sound like I'm seventy*—in high school and the type of bond we all had. I mean it is still here, it's just after every day it is harder and harder to see. I used to write so much, not essays but songs, stories, poems; I wish I could remember them all. I wish I could remember music…. I remember vivid stuff but not much. Sometimes while working or thinking, I'll catch myself singing lyrics from an old song from before. I know not MUCH time has passed, but so much has happened that it feels like ten years when it's only been about three. The pen and paper, the computer, the free expression, that was my escape from the world, my way of being able to express everything in just a few lines, but since this happened I have no more inspiration for them. We take for granted the little things we are given that we don't think about living without, but once you go without, you realize the privilege and the opportunities you were given. Don't get me wrong, there is so much I could say, but it's like all my dreams, desires, and motivation are disappearing. And I don't know if I can catch it and write it down on paper anymore. I don't even think I would know where to start. I finally head back down and see Alex sitting alone and Miko and Jordan talking. "Why are you over here?" I ask.

"I know we need that guy here, but I don't like him," he answers.

"Why?" I ask.

"There is a vibe about him. You know I'm good at reading people," he says.

"I mean, you're not wrong." I laugh slightly.

"And after how you guys said he treated Allison, it's just hard to like him," he says, and he makes a good point. I don't know how Miko can sit and talk to him with a straight face. "Plus, I don't want to seem like a jealous boyfriend, because I'm not," he says.

"I understand completely. Just try to be on your best behavior," I tell him, and Allison comes out and immediately comes and sits down with us and avoids talking or looking in the direction of Jordan. "Heyyy." I smile at her, and she plasters a fake smile across her face.

"Hi," she says coldly.

As if things couldn't get worse, Jordan comes over and sits across from Allison. Alex gets up and leaves. "Hey, Miranda, and hey, Allison." He smiles. Something about his smile seems off, like genuine, but a scary kind of genuine. He knows he messed up, but he also knows he still has a hold on Allison in a way no one will understand. He was emotionally abusive and controlling and broke Allison so fast and hard it surprised her.

"Uh, hey," I say.

"What's your friend's problem with me?" he asked.

"Well—" I get cut off. OH MY GOD, THIS GIRL NEVER LETS ME SPEAK!

"Maybe because your presence isn't wanted," Allison snaps at him.

"Damn, I'm sorry. I thought everyone was cool with me staying here," he jokes.

"It's not that, it just takes time to adjust," I say.

"Look, Allison, I'm sorry. I know we didn't end on the perfect terms, but I want to catch up if that's okay. I'm not saying go out, obviously, but just try to talk more." I side-eye him, and he shifts uncomfortably. "I wanna know how you guys have been, I wanna know how YOU personally have been. Just think about it, okay? I won't bother you guys anymore. Goodnight." Jordan stands up and walks away.

I hear Alex fake cough. "Fake asshole."

"Alex!" Miko says.

"I'm sorry," he apologizes, and Allison and I laugh at overhearing them.

"Hey, how are you feeling?" I ask, concerned.

"Honestly? I'm confused as hell, and it's not like I hate him, I can't hate anyone." I raise an eyebrow. "Yes, the feelings for him are gone, you jealous little baby." She laughs, and I shrug. "Anyhow, I don't think I want to talk to him…at least not right now," she says. I get why she feels that way. I'm not even sure if I want her to talk to him.

"That makes sense. You take all the time you need, okay?" I tell her.

"Thanks. I'm gonna head to bed. Goodnight" she says and kisses my cheek and walks away.

"I feel like a clown in the goddamn circus," I mumble, and I hear Miko laugh. "You hear me?" I ask, and she nods. "It's true!" She just laughs again. "Go do your lookout with Alex!" I yell. From now on, keep the thoughts in your head, Miranda.

*   *   *

The next morning I spent a few extra hours sleeping in because I was physically exhausted. By the time I woke up, everyone was doing their own thing, and I didn't like that. We looked separate yet together. I noticed Allison and Jordan having a very awkward conversation. I can tell by the way Allison keeps shifting back and forth and hesitating her answers. "Good morning," I walk over and say to the both of them. I see Allison's attitude shift completely.

"Morning," she says and hugs me.

"Hey, Miranda. Totallyyy not trying to be rude, but we are trying to talk," Jordan says sarcastically. *Ughhhhh.* I walk away before I say anything aggressive or rude, but Allison grabs my wrist.

"She can stay," she says.

"No, don't worry." I fake a smile.

"Yeah, I need her anyway!" Alex says; you can hear the anger hidden in his voice. I get that he doesn't like the guy either, but he doesn't need to make anything worse. I need to reprimand this kid or I'll get Miko on his ass.

"Alex, rooms, now," I tell him. "I'll be back, and don't worry, won't interrupt again." I walk into the room and see Alex already waiting.

"I don't like that guy. I feel like he is trying to manipulate her," he says.

"I get it, but you aren't going to make it better by acting like you have a stick up your ass," I tell him. "Look, I don't like him here as much as you do, but try to be civilized. We don't need anything else bad happening, okay?" I ask, and he nods. "Thank you." We hug it out. I hear someone come into the school crying.

Allison comes into the room and hugs me tightly. "I miss my family," she cries. *What the fuck goes on when I'm not there?* I thought.

"What happened?" I asked.

"Jordan and I started talking about the past and it just didn't sit well for me," she mumbled.

"Alex…" I trail off.

"Say no more, my friend." He walks out.

"Tell Miko to start cooking!" He gives a thumbs up. "Now, here, sit." I help her sit on the bed.

"I just miss how life was before…. Yeah, it was stressful, but everyone wasn't dead or dying. Like yes, I have you and Miko and Alex, but it is just so different," she says.

"I feel like that too. I wish I could rewind time. I wish we all didn't lose so much. Hell, I wish we still weren't losing. But all we can do is just keep living, and if we can't live for us, then we live for those we lost. We live in this world until we die, we just keep going," I tell her, and her crying slows down. I let her calm down a little more before speaking again. "Why don't you take a nap?" I suggest, and she nods and lies down. I wait a second, then get up and go to my room and sit waiting for dinner.

This world sucks.… I get it isn't supposed to be easy, but, god, why does it have to be so hard? The next morning, I make Alex sit with all of us and I let Allison sleep in because I know she had a very hard time sleeping. No one is talking. Right now we are eating in such high tension and thick and heavy with awkwardness that it feels like it's choking me. I know I'm not the only one who doesn't feel this heaviness, since Miko isn't smiling. Alex has his fist clenched under the table, and Jordan is on the opposite side of the same table. "Shouldn't you wake up Allison? She's been sleeping for a while," Jordan asked.

"Don't worry about it. I'll wake her up when I wake her up," I tell him.

"Maybe if you didn't make her cry she would be up and ready," Alex mumbles, and Miko kicks him under the table. "Everyone knows that I am right," he says.

"Alex!" Miko yells.

"Shut up, man," I tell him

"What did you say?" Jordan asks.

"Nothing important," I tell him.

"If you heard me then you heard me; if you didn't, you didn't." Alex pushes his plate aside. "I suddenly don't want to eat anymore. Miranda, when you need me, I'll be in the gym." He walks away.

"Don't listen to him," Miko tells him.

"He is being a dick. Like, I didn't do anything to him," Jordan says.

"I know. He just doesn't take newcomers lightly," I try to explain.

"I don't care, he's starting to get me mad," Jordan says and gets up "If you guys don't want problems, tell your friend to relax." He walks away.

"Well…" Miko trails off.

"I'm gonna go wake her up," I say. I get up and walk away. Alex is such a bratty toddler sometimes I swear. I knock on Allison's door. "Can I come in?" No answer. "Allison?" Still no answer. I open the door, and no one is here.

I look around her room; her bag is gone, her clothes, products, and even her sentimental stuffed animal that she still has is gone. I see a folded note on her desk that says, *"I'm sorry."* I pick it up and open it up. It says…

First, let me say it again. I'm sorry, but I just had to leave, Miranda… Please forgive me. I know you won't want to forgive me, but please let me explain first… . I left in the middle of the night, when I know you usually fall asleep on your post even when you don't mean to. Yes, that's how long I have been planning my leave. I just had to wait for the right moment. I love all of you, and I was honored to be co-person in charge. Miko, Alex, I love you guys, just keep pushing and don't ever give up on the family. You guys witnessed firsthand everything that has been happening. I know you guys have feelings too, and please don't box them in, because they won't lead to anything good, I swear. Please promise me you guys will speak up. I know if I tried to leave in the daytime you guys would have just stopped me again, but I know I had to go. I don't think it was just Jordan that made me want to leave (even though he played a huge part in it), I just don't feel like I'm worthy enough to be with you guys, and I can't stand to watch and lose another one of you (especially you, Miranda). Yes, him being there caused my anxiety to go up and my decision-making skills to go down, but I just don't think I am strong or wise enough. You guys will be just fine without me there. You guys have Miranda, but she needs to remember she has you guys too. I am thankful for how far we have come as a group and as a family. To be honest, after the day of Kevin's dying, I couldn't stomach losing another one of you guys. Then what I did to Victoria… And Justin. I can't even sleep a full night. My nightmares take control over me, and I become that same evil and devilish person I was in that moment all over again. I'm scared that my nightmares will become reality. I need to leave before I hurt one of you guys again, better yet I need to leave before I lose you guys. I rather cause pain a little now than a lot more in the long run. Just know that I will never ever forget you guys. I have something that reminds me of all of you guys with me at all times. Just remember, we weren't blood, but I loved you guys just like, if not MORE than any family. Maybe in time I will see you guys again. I'm gonna be just fine, Miranda. Please don't come and look for me. I'll be okay.

No…no…no! My head starts to get really dizzy and the room starts spinning. Why did she leave? I can't tell anyone; they can't know she is gone. What am I gonna do? "I…I can't b-breathe." I start gasping and sit down on the floor. I can't lose another person! Especially not her. She helped me stay grounded, she keeps me sane, she… She was everything I needed. *I'll be okay.* That never ends well. I start crying harder than I have since my family died. Maybe I failed. I should have tried harder to make her feel better! Maybe I should have just kicked Jordan out. This is all my fault. "I…n-need to t-talk to t-the o-others." I start to stand up but my legs and hands are shaking too much to grip on to the dresser and force myself up. I try again, but this time I fall and scarp my arm on an edge of the bed. "Ow, f-fuck." I grab my arm. Calm down, Miranda… Calm down… Try to, please. IT'S NOT WORKING! Tears keep falling down my face like a waterfall; my body is shaking faster than a damn earthquake. I'm breathing erratically, and now my arm is gushing blood. I try to get up, and this time I can stand, but my body is still shaking really bad, and now I'm dripping blood after every step I take. I walk out the room still dizzy, but this time it's a mixture of the aching pain of her leaving and the loss of blood. "G-guys.. HE-HELP!" I try to yell.

"Miranda!" Alex yells. He and Miko run to me. I almost drop to the floor, but Alex grabs me and picks me up.

"Come, I gotta stitch her up," I hear Miko say. I see Jordan just sitting at the picnic table staring at me, not in horror, not in joy; I'm not sure how he is looking at me. All I know is he isn't helping.

Miko stitches my arm up and bandages it. "Do we have to babyproof everything now?" she jokes, and I just smile and stretch my arm out. It feels like I just slit my wrist…. I shiver at the bad memories.

"I'm okay," I tell her.

"Hey, where is Allison?" Jordan says.

"You can't be considerate for one second or has your heart gone completely selfish?" Alex says.

"Guys…" Miko trails off

"Bro, shut up. No one's even talking to you," Jordan says and rolls his eyes.

"Why don't you try to make me shut up." Alex stands face to face with Jordan.

"Stop acting like little fucking boys!" I yell.

"You're right, Miranda… I'm sorry that your friend is bad at timing," Jordan says.

"You're the one who is being inconsiderate," Alex says.

"Miranda just said stop fighting. Listen to her," Jordan says. The tension should be diminishing, but instead, it feels like it is rising.

"I don't need to listen to you," Alex says.

I swear, this guy's anger issues. But now, time seems to slow down as everything plays out. Alex is still standing face to face with Jordan, and then Jordan shoves Alex, and Alex punches Jordan in his gut, causing Jordan to bend over and fall to the floor.

"Cheap shot," Jordan coughs out.

"Wanna see cheap you mother—", Alex starts to speak, but I stop him.

I grab Alex by his arm. "Go for a walk." I push him out of the room. "Now!" I yell, and he walks away. "You good?" I hold my good arm's hand out, but he doesn't take it and stands up on his own.

"Fine," he says.

"I should uhh…make sure Alex is okay." Miko is about to leave.

"Tell him to come in, sit down, and play nice, please… It's important," I sigh and say to Jordan. "That goes for you too." Miko goes and gets Alex, Jordan and I just sit there in awkward silence.

"So, how's your stomach?" I ask.

"Good, good. How is your arm?" he asks.

"Oh, it's good," I answered. This conversation is more awkward than when you try to explain sex to kindergarteners. I mean why would you be…NOT THE POINT! It's also drier than dinner last night…. No offense to Miko.

She walks in with Alex. "Please try to play nice," she tells him. He sits in the chair in the corner. So, how do I tell them this? How do I tell them that our best friend is gone? How can I tell them that the whole backbone of us…? Another one of the people that we love is just up and disappeared. The person that helped us all still be living, who always had the ideas and logic…left?

"You're scaring us, Miranda," Alex says hesitantly.

"Yeah, please tell us," Miko says.

"This isn't gonna be easy…" I trail off. "About Allison…she is gone, guys. She left with all her things…. I don't know where she went." I show them the letter, and Miko starts crying. Alex just stays silent.

"How did she slip by? Why were you sleeping on your shift?" Jordan asked, and honestly, he is right, I am the common denominator for everything bad that happens. I wish I knew how to end that in a different way from how I am thinking.

"You try working, hunting, and cleaning all day long and then pulling all-nighters. Read the letter. It says how my body gives out and crashes sometimes," I try to explain, but he just doesn't seem to care. I get that he cares and is worried about Allison...we all are. I get it, it is all my fault, it is always my fault. But there are better ways to go around and say it.

"We have to go look for her!" Miko says.

"Yeah!" Alex says.

"No, guys," I interrupt. "I know it is killing you guys almost as much as it's killing me when it comes to this situation, but we can't go after her," I say.

"But why!" Miko asked.

"If we go out and find her, then what? She still doesn't come with us? She hates us? I hate to admit this, guys, but this was her choice, not ours. We need to respect it." My heart sank having to say those words, but I know it's what she wants. When it comes to Allison you have to let her feel how she feels alone. If she tells you to "leave her alone" or "it's nothing," then you have to drop it. I know we all don't want to admit it, but they ALL know I'm right.

"Ugh, you're right," Alex says. "I need to go do something to get my mind off of this. I'm taking my lookout shift early," Alex tells everyone and walks off.

"Do you two wanna go to the fishing ground?" I ask, and they both nod. "Let's go, then."

We walk in silence the whole way there, people nervous to bring up, every topic is just so miserable now. When we arrive at the river, I just sit there. I don't grab the spears, I don't tell them to. I just sit and watch the fish swim against the current. Miko comes and sits next to me. "What's on your mind?" she asks.

"God, so much," I say, and she just looks at me sadly. "I miss Allison so much…. Yeah, I miss Justin and Victoria too, it's just different with Allison…. Really different," I say. I never had "best friends" because those words just never turned out good for me. Justin was, I guess you can say, a best friend, *even though I prefer not to*, and Allison was, well, you know…my girlfriend, who always seemed to be there for me…*always.*

"Are we gonna fish or like just chill? I'm good either way," Jordan says, and I just roll my eyes.

"Spears are under those bushes. You go see if you can get at least three fish for tonight," I tell him, and he goes off to do it.

"I wish we had purpose," I start off.

"Wait, what?" she asks.

"Just think about it for a second," I tell her.

"What do you mean?" Miko asks.

"Like we were put on this earth to breathe, live, and die when it's your time to go and whatever you do within that time is up to you. But now we breathe, live, and die but with one key word: we survive. We survive and survive, just to die anyway. And now, unfortunately, we have a very high chance of becoming one of those things…. We will be forgotten, you are always forgotten," I say, and Miko stares at me in shock. "I'm sorry. I didn't mean to ramble," I apologize.

"You don't have to say you're sorry," Miko reassures. "It's just scary how accurate that was," she says.

"I know. I have a pretty dark mindset," I tell her.

"Don't we all nowadays?" Miko says.

After about another twenty minutes Jordan comes back. "Caught five," he says.

"Perfect, let's head home," I say. The walk back wasn't as awkward as walking to, but still, no one said a word. When we arrive, I signal for Alex to come downstairs. "Miko, go start cooking, Jordan, go look out, and Alex, I don't know, go find something to do." I go sit down and pull out Allison's note again and begin rereading it until dinner is done.

After dinner, Alex was half asleep, and Miko too. I get it, they are tired, but I'm also an asshole. So I shoved Alex's head into a bowl. I only just wake Miko up. She is weird to try and prank. "All jokes aside, guys, we are running low on medicine, bandages, and some other supplies, so we need to go out and hunt/raid tomorrow. We all will be going, that is all," I tell them.

Let's see what happens, right? I really, really don't want to go outside, especially with the two crying babies. I head to my room, since Jordan said he wanted to do the shift tonight, and I look around and notice my favorite snapback was gone. I brought a little bag full of sentimentals with me. I guess Allison took it. I know she always liked it; at least she has something to remember me. As I lie in my bed, I just stare up at the ceiling and just wonder how it would be if we went to college or were able to pursue a real life. Why does our generation have to suffer? I'm not saying olders aren't, but why do the younger and the ones to come have to deal with this? Who is to say we make it long enough to make another generation? We *won't be okay* was the last thing I thought before falling asleep.

We won't be okay...

The next morning everyone wakes up in a surprisingly good mood. No, they are not jolly like freaking Santa Claus, but they aren't at each other's throats. Unless that's what they are into...anyway. "Hey," I say to Miko as I grab an apple.

"Morning." She smiles.

"Hey, Alex." I hug him.

"Hey, Miranda," he says.

I look over and see Jordan sitting by himself, and even though I am an asshole, I am not heartless. "Hey, Jordan. How was your shift?" I ask, and he looks up at me very confused. I don't blame him.

"Oh, um, it was a quiet night. Thanks for asking." He half-smiles at me.

"Miranda, I need your help." Alex pulls me away in a hurry.

"What?" I ask.

"I made a note for Miko, but I don't know how to give it to her." He hands it to me.

"Are we back in fucking elementary? Is this 'if you like me check yes or no' thing? Because you're already dating her." I laugh.

"No! I'm not good at telling people how I feel in person, so I wrote it down," he says. Yep, definitely back in elementary.

"Fine, I'll give it to her." I roll my eyes and go to Miko. "This is from your dummy of a boyfriend." I hand her the note.

"Thanks?" she questions. I leave her bed and go off finishing my apple. I walk to our little "cemetery" and look at the names one by one and replay each death in my head. I really hope we don't have to add a name anytime soon... Please let her be okay.

I give everyone a chance to finish eating before speaking "Okay! Guys, we need to head out now!" I yell.

"What are we waiting for then?" Alex says.

"Let's go," I tell them, and we leave. We all went out again. We figured we live together, then we die together. Plus, it's more helpful. "Do you guys wanna go back to that house we went to last time?" I asked.

"Wouldn't that be empty?" Alex asked.

"Not necessarily. We didn't check everywhere. There was still a basement and other rooms, remember?" I tell him, and he nods. We follow the same trail we took last time and eventually reach the house. "Boom." I point. "Fuck, guys, look." I point again and see six zombies around the house.

"Let's just shoot them," Jordan suggests.

"No, are you crazy!" I whisper/yell. "We will draw way too much noise. We need to be quiet and careful," I tell them.

"So how is this going down, then?" Jordan asked. Man, sometimes I wanna just pluck him in his head.

"Alex, you go for the two on the left, I'll go for the two on the right, and each of you go for one of the ones in the front. Got it?" Everyone nods and pulls out their "silent" weapon. I motion one…two…three, and we all take off running. I stab the first one in the side of its head, then the second I kick in its leg. *Ouch, bad memories.* And stab it in its forehead, twice. "Everyone clear?" I see Jordan and Miko standing there, and they nod, then I turn and see Alex standing up from killing his second one.

"Ready when you are," Miko says. I open the door and it looks clear.

"Okay, this time I'll look in the bathrooms. Alex, double check the kitchen. Miko, the rooms, and Jordan, check the basement," I tell them.

"Why do I have to go to the dark and dingy basement?" Jordan asked.

"Because the non-important one has to do the shitty jobs," Alex says.

"Alex!" Miko and I say.

"Alex, don't be so rude," Miko says.

"Okay, it's true th—" I cut him off by glaring. "I'm just sorry," he finishes.

"Anyway. It's because I said so. Now go," I tell them, and we all split up. I check the bathroom on the first floor and find toilet paper, bandages, ointments and other creams, and painkillers. "Perfect," I whispered. I know a girl in this day and age must be dying every month. I look around one more time but don't find anything else useful. I go up to check the second-floor bathroom, and in there I find more painkillers, thread and needles, rubbing alcohol, cotton balls, and pads/tampons. "Guess girls lived here," I say. I wonder if only girls lived here. Would it be as crazy as people think it would? I mean I don't think so; if you don't wanna talk or in a mood then just walk away. I kind of sound hypocritical… Oh well!

"Miranda!" I hear Miko yell. I immediately pull out my gun. *Please let everything be okay.*

I run into the room she yelled from and stop short. "Oh my god! Y-you're okay!" I stuttered out. I go and hug Allison tightly.

"I told you guys not to follow me," she says, hugging me back.

"We didn't, we came to raid the house," Miko says.

I pull back from the hug and grab Allison's hands. "Please, please come back with us," I beg.

"I don't think I should." She sighs.

"Please, we all miss you so much. I thought you were dead, and now that I know you're not, I don't wanna leave here without you," I tell her.

"Some of us miss you more than others," Miko points out, and we all laugh.

"I guess that—"

"I found alcohol!" Jordan yells.

"Let's go make sure they are okay down there," I say. "You coming?" I ask, and she takes my hand and nods.

We go downstairs and Jordan has two bottles in his bag and two in his hand. "Holy shit, Allison is back," Jordan points out, completely ignoring Allison and me holding hands.

"Allison, you're alive," Alex says.

"Yeah…" she trails off.

"I'm glad you're okay." Alex smiles, and Jordan rolls his eyes. "Anyway, what are in the bottles?" Alex asked.

"Oh, two are bottles of wine. One is whiskey and one is vodka," Jordan says. "Let's go back and party!"

"I am so down. I call the first shot, though," I say.

"Really?" Allison says. "We shouldn't get too crazy, guys."

"We aren't even of age yet," Miko chimes in.

"Yeah, because there are a bunch of bartenders, cops, and laws that have legal states anymore," I tell them.

"This would just be a typical day for me, I'm in," Alex says.

"Perfect, so we are drinking. Now let's get back," I say as we leave.

"I don't like this," Miko says.

"Yeah, well, you never like anything," I joke. As we head back to school, Allison and I start to trail behind. "So…" I say.

"So?" she questions

"Do you have my hat?" I ask, and she rolls her eyes and pulls that hat out of the bag and puts it on my head.

"There." She laughs.

"Okay, now a serious question. Are you staying?" I ask. I can tell she is very hesitant to answer this question.

"Yes…at least I think so," she answers. Up ahead we see two zombies approaching. "Miko and Jordan, get them," she tells them, and they kill both of the zombies with ease. Jordan goes and directly stabs his in the head, Miko sweeps the leg of hers before stabbing it in the forehead.

"Not even back twenty minutes and already giving demands," I say.

"Shhhh." She puts a finger to her lips.

"Finally, we are back! Let's have some drinks," Alex says.

"We should play truth or dare, while drinking," I suggest.

"Awesome," Jordan says.

"But the rule is, everyone must drink at least one cup of something tonight, and everyone gets one chance to say no," I say, and everyone nods.

"Now, let's have some fun," Jordan says, putting all four bottles on the table and pulling out glasses. "What does everyone want?"

"Wine," Allison says.

"A mix of vodka and whiskey," Alex asks.

"Same for me," I tell him.

"I don't really want anything…" Miko says.

"Come on, it will be fun! Just have a cup of wine," Jordan says, pouring all the drinks.

"First dare to start everything: let's see who could chug their drink faster!" I say. "Ready…set…go!" We all start chugging our drinks, and right before I'm about to slam my cup down, Alex slams his down on the table.

"Done!" he says

"Fuck, I was so close." I roll my eyes.

"Well, you win some, you lose some," he says, pouring himself and me another cup of what we just drank and pouring Allison another cup of wine.

"Alex, be careful, I don't think you should drink too much," Miko says.

"Don't worry, babe." He holds his cup up.

"Jordan?" I motion, but I can see he has the other bottle of wine all to himself and he is just drinking from that. "Anyway, Alex, you can ask the first question," I tell him.

"Okay, Miko, truth or dare?" Of course he chooses her.

"Truth," she answers.

Boringgggggg.

"Worst thing you have ever done?" he asked; this time we each go for a shot of vodka.

"You guys really shouldn't be drinking so much, but the worst thing I have done is probably cut class," she says.

"You are the most boring bad girl everrr." I laugh.

"Take it easy." Allison grabs my cup from me. "No more for at least two rounds." Ugh she is acting like a mom; maybe she needs to get drunk. No, I can't have drunk Allison and drunk Miranda and drunk everyone, it will be chaos. But still, not cool.

"But…but…Allison," I whine.

"Not now, please." She places her hand over mine for a second. Definitely not just friends. "You can have some later."

"Whatever." I huff and stare at Jordan who seems to just downing that bottle really fast.

"Allison, truth or dare?" Miko asks.

"Let's go for a dare." She takes a sip of her drink.

"I dare you to drink what is in Miranda's cup," Miko says.

"Ew, this is dumb strong though… Fine." She drinks the rest of my cup and gags. I don't think I ever saw Allison drink. I mean I never gotten drunk, but I picked up a glass or two before. But her and Miko, nope. But my cup isn't that baddddd, she is exaggerating…. I want my drink! I…want…my… drink! "You have to wait." Oops I guess I said that out loud instead of in my head. "My turn. Miranda, truth or dare?" she says.

"Uhhhh, truth," I say. I don't wanna do her dare, it might be boring.

"Okay, share your first-kiss experience," she says.

"My first kiss was with a boy in third grade who had a HUGE crush on me and it was actually a dare… Then we dated for two months." Everyone laughs, even Jordan. "Can I have a drink now?" I ask, and she nods, pouring me a cup. "Jordan, you are too quiet right now, so truth or dare?" I ask.

"Dare," he slurs. Damn, he is the most drunk out of all of us.

"I dare you to chug the rest of that bottle" He has at least a quarter left.

"Fine." Sure enough, he chugs the rest. "I think I'm going to—" He cuts himself off by puking in the bushes. I laugh and pour just whiskey into a cup. I'm *going light now.*

*   *   *

About twenty minutes later and boy, are Alex, Jordan, and I are bombed out of our minds! Miko is like ninety-eight percent sober, Allison is asleep with her head on the table because she is a high key lightweight, and us three are doneeeee. Somehow, Alex is only in his underwear, I think from a dare, Jordan has his shoes off, and I just reek of alcohol "I…I don't remember whose turn it is," I say.

"It's yours," Miko says.

"Alex, truth or dare?" I say.

"Dare!" He flexes, what he is flexing? I have no idea.

"Alex!" Miko laughs. Aww, they are cute. He throws her little hand guns…now they are just corny.

"I dare you to draw on your stomach." I hand him a Sharpie. "With your eyes shut"

"No problem." He closes his eyes and draws a big smiley face on his stomach. It actually came out pretty good, just that one of the smile lines is connected to an eye. "Jordan, wait…oh, truth or dare!" Alex says.

"Truth." Jordan is like, half asleep right now.

"Is Allison a good kisser?" He winks at me and I flip him off.

"Why does that concern you?" Jordan seems to immediately sober up, in an angry drunk way, and he is no longer half-awake. Me, on the other hand… What game were we playing? Oh, never mind, it's the truth or dare.

"I'm asking for a friend," Alex holds his hands up in defense.

"Yeah? What friend?" Jordan says.

"If you don't know then you are one bliiiiind son of a bitch." Alex laughs.

"You shouldn't need to know if she is a good kisser or not. You aren't going to be kissing her." Damn, Jordan sounds really jealous right now. I didn't exactly take him for that. I guess drunk mouths really do speak sober thoughts.

"I don't want to start problems with you, Jordan," Alex says.

"Why are you asking, then?" he asks.

"Because, you dumbass, if you couldn't see, they aren't exactly a couple, but Miranda and Allison are *real* close!" Alex points to us. "I'm dating Miko!"

"Guys! You are both wayyy too drunk for this," Miko says. What a nice person she is, always trying to have peace.

"I'm not," Alex starts to sway slightly back and forth, and Jordan uses that as an advantage to tackle Alex to the ground.

"Ooouuu… Fight! Fight! Fight!" I chant. Usually I would break this up, but nah, I don't wanna move. Plus…what was I saying? Never mind.

"Shhhh, you're too loud." Allison covers my mouth with her hand, and I laugh and bite her hand. "Ouch!" She pulls it back.

"Not sorry," I say, and she shakes her head and this time puts her arms around my neck as well. Drunk her is way touchier than sober her. Now back to the fight!

Jordan punches Alex in the face, but Alex retaliates and pushes Jordan off; watching these two fight right now is funnier than funny. Alex punches Jordan again and again, but Miko is able to pull Alex off. "Stop!" Miko yells. Damn, she's loud as hell. Alex stops and tumbles back into his chair and ends up passing out from what I am assuming is the alcohol. "Jordan, you okay?" she asks, and Jordan wipes the blood from his nose and nods.

"Yeah…I need to sleep, though." Instead of getting up, he stays on the ground and falls asleep. Most anti-climactic fight ever.

"You gonna stay here?" she asks, and I nod.

"I'm wayyyy too out of it to move." I laugh and put my head down on the table. Before Miko walks off, I yell to her, "We can never play games in this group!" I hear her laugh a little.

The next morning I wake up with the world's worst headache, but now I know what a hangover feels like, a sore neck, and almost no memory of last night. I look around and see Jordan on the floor, Alex on a chair, and

Miko and Allison cooking and laughing. "Ahhh, someone is up finally," Allison says, handing me two painkillers and water. "What a wild night, right?" She and Miko laugh.

"Yeah, it's so much fun to see me suffer." I groan, and they laugh more.

"You know we are just playing, M." Allison sits with me and hands me some food.

"I smell food." Alex wakes up and grabs himself a plate. How the hell is this boy perfectly fine? Jordan wakes up a couple seconds after, and when he gets up, Alex and him have a really mean staring contest.

Ohh, the fight that happened! "This should be fun," I whisper, but instead of another brawl happening, they walk right past each other. Don't they hate each other? I mean I'm not mad, less yelling I have to do with a hangover. Memories of last night are kind of fuzzy but I know not to dare ask anyone. Last night was fun, though. It's good to get your mind off of all the dark, heavy, and deadly stuff every once in a while. It just sucks that night like that has to happen in order for me to be happy again, to make me actually wanna be here. Don't get me wrong, I am happy with Allison, and I'm happy that our group is still somewhat alive, but I can never be truly happy again. I don't even think I was in the first place. I wasn't happy before this started, so how can I be happy after? I'm a lost cause that is breathing. "Stupid thoughts," I mumble to myself; if only I could lock my mind away and throw away the key.

After breakfast we all kind of feel a little sick and sore from yesterday, so we decided that today would be our day off. I immediately go to my room and lie in my bed and stare at my ceiling. "Hey, can I come in?" Miko asks while poking her head through the door, and I nod. "I was thinking we all should look at the graveyard today," she suggests.

"Why?" Great, make me feel better.

"I don't know, I just feel like we are forgetting that we are family. That we are still alive, that just because some of our friends and family aren't with us anymore doesn't mean we forget we have each other. We are supposed to be able to work together without arguing, I just think it might help us," she says.

"It's like giving us a reality check?" I ask.

"Yeah, sorta like that I guess." She shrugs.

"That...that isn't such a bad idea. I'll go get everyone's attention and we can go in about ten minutes." I get up and go outside. The only one out here is Allison. I go up to her. "Boo!" She jumps slightly. "Miko thought it would be a good idea if we ALL go to the gravesite together."

"That is a good idea. Let me guess, you want me to tell everyone?" Allison says.

"Bingo," I joke. "No, I'll do it." I go and find Jordan and Alex *not at the same time* and tell them to meet us at the site in ten.

Once everyone is together, we go and see the names of the ones we lost, and no one says a word. Allison stares at Victoria's and Justin's names with tears in her eyes, Alex and Jordan have their heads down, and Miko is just standing there as if she is just letting herself get lost in the moment of looking back and forth between the names. Me? Well, I can't stop looking at Kevin's name. I'm the first one to move a muscle. I run my hand across Kevin's name and replay the memories we had in my head. I don't like that you guys are gone, but I won't let this group fail. We need to be a family again, whether we are standing here right now or our name is on that wall, we ARE family…. That will never change.

Allison was the first one to say, "I'm so sorry, guys." She starts crying.

"For what? You didn't do anything," I say. Now all eyes are on her and I'm not sure she wants that.

"I…I need a minute." She runs off, and before Jordan or anyone goes after her, I stop them.

"Let her go," I say.

"No," Jordan says, trying to get past me. Why does this guy always have to be so difficult!

"I'm not asking, I'm telling," I tell him. "As a matter of fact, it's an order." I don't like abusing my "power" like this, but if it means the person in need is okay, I'll do anything.

"Ugh, fine." He rolls his eyes and walks away. I get it, my dude, but goddamn.

I let Allison be for a few minutes, and just as I'm about to go talk to her, she comes outside. "Are you okay?" Miko asks, and Allison nods with a smile.

"Good," I say, and we all sit together. Alex and Jordan are sitting at the same table. Holy shit, someone take a mental note…not really because they are on two different ends again. After a little while, I jump up. "You know what would be fun?" I say, and everyone just looks at me, confused. "Why don't we all get off our asses and do something predictive? Because in case any of you forgot, we are in the apocalypse and have to be ready for anything. We have been slacking off and being petty, and it's really annoying. So, Miko, you and I are gonna do some training; Allison, you can go check on the green house with Alex; and Jordan, go do something and make yourself useful," I say, and everyone gets up and goes off.

"Why didn't you have Allison train with you?" Miko asks.

"Because...I don't know." I shrug. "Now, use your bow and arrow and shoot the target from... Here." I guide her to a spot. She lines up and shoots the target. "Not bullseye, try one more time," I say, and she tries again, this time getting closer.

"I can usually hit that!" She sighs in frustration.

"If you keep your back arm relaxed and stop thinking so much, you can hit it," Jordan pops in.

Great, the peanut gallery is here.

Miko tries again and hits the target closer than before. "Thank you," she tells him. Allison and Alex come back with a basket of apples.

"Great, now we all never need to see doctors again," I joke.... No one laughs.

"Bad joke, sis," Alex says, and I roll my eyes and grab one.

"It was good, just not original," Allison says. "You have made better ones." I flip her off.

"You guys are dicks. Just because of that, Alex and Allison, you guys can join me on the hunting grounds today. Let's go." I smirk.

"Why can't I come?" Miko says.

"You can come," Allison decides.

"But—" I try to intervene but she just ignores me.

"Uhh, what about me?" Jordan asked.

"You stay and watch the school. We will be back," I say, and he nods.

We all head out into the woods; it probably wasn't the best day to go out. There was a lot more zombies out this night than usual, but we need to eat something. "Look," Allison whispers and points to a group of zombies. Past the zombies I see a dog. Am I really about to kill a dog? Unfortunately, yes.

"I can't use my gun, it will be too loud. Wait here, guys." I pull out my dagger, and right before I'm about to get up, Allison grabs my shoulder.

"Are you crazy?" she whispers/yells. "It's too dangerous, Miranda," she tells me.

"I'll be fine." I look at the group. "If I'm not back in five, leave."

"Miranda…" Allison trails.

"Leave," I say and get up and hide behind a tree. "I need to create a diversion," I whisper to myself. I look all around right where I'm standing and find a rock. I pick it up and chuck the rock onto another tree on the opposite side and it seems to catch their attention. Once the last one is moving, I run up and stab the dog three times, killing it. To my surprise, it barked the first time, and a couple of the zombies turned around. "Fuck…" I say and pick up the dog. I run back to where the other three were hiding and pass the dog to Alex.

Allison hugs me tightly. "You're okay." She hugs me tighter.

"I told you I would be fine." I laugh and hug her back. "All this aside, we should get back before it gets any darker," I say, pulling back.

We make it back to the school and find Jordan fiddling with his pistol right in front of the fire. "I'll, um, start cooking," Miko says.

"What the fuck are you doing?" I ask Jordan.

"I have one bullet left," he says. "I'm trying to determine how I want to use it." He looks up. "Let's play Russian Roulette." Everyone goes silent and stunned, not knowing what to say.

"Are you fucking crazy?" Alex says, and honestly, I don't blame him for his outburst comment.

"Really, Jordan? You want to play a game that could kill one of us? We need all the manpower we can get," I tell him, and try to get the gun from his hand, but he snatches it back. I try again, and this time I grab it and try to pull it out of his hand, but he won't let go.

Alex pushes Jordan down, making his grip on the gun slip. "She said get off." Alex clenches his fist.

"We will play that game eventually, watch." Jordan stands up and points at all of us. "When you all get so depressed, not knowing whether you hate or love each other anymore. Trying to decide if it is even worth it to keep going or give up in this world of hell. Don't you get it! Just you wait and see." Jordan tells everyone and storms off into the building. Again, we all just stand there in silence, and this time I'm not sure if it is a surprising silence or not. I try to examine everyone's facial features, but everyone is just stoned face. It is like we are trying to read each other and hide our own feelings in the process. Could Jordan have a point? Is there a point where we are just so broken that the pieces are scattered forever? Suicide, I guess. That's the point of no return, that's the point when you are so damaged that there's the only conclusion. I'll admit I have thought about just ending it, on more than one occasion, more than usual recently, but I can't. I have to be strong for my family here, because, without them all here together, I have nothing.

It's been a good five minutes and still no one moved until Allison speaks up. "Guys, the food is starting to burn." She points at the fire.

"Oh! I'll get right on that," Miko says and walks off.

"I'll, um, help her." Alex looks between Allison and me and follows Miko.

"Let's go talk up on the lookout stand," I say, and she nods as we climb up to the spot. At first, we don't say anything and count all the zombies that are in the distance. There aren't as many as yesterday, but unfortunately, it doesn't mean anything. "So…how have you been feeling?"

"Horrible, I've been replaying what Jordan said in my head, and he really has a point," she tells me. "I love you guys, and I don't want anything to happen to you guys, but maybe the game would be a good idea," she says. Is she serious! Why in the world would she want to risk her life, Miko and Alex's lives… My life.

"You want to play the game!" I say. "Why in the world would you want to risk it, Allison!" I yell.

"I'm not saying to do it, I'm just saying to think about it." She shrugs and looks at me.

"I can't believe you." I shake my head. "I can't talk to you right now." I get down and storm into Jordan's room.

"Woah, privacy," he tells me. Like he gets any privacy.

"You need to leave," I tell him.

"Why?" he asked me.

"You're fucking up everything here. Don't you forget, you're just a liability whose time just ran out, and to top it all off, you bring up the dumb idea that could kill someone here!" I shout and point my gun at him. "How about I kill you right now."

"Woah." He gasps and holds his hands up. "Take it easy." He stands up slowly.

"Sit the fuck down!" I shoot the wall next to him.

"This is exactly what I'm talking about, Miranda," he starts. "Think about it, you're cracking. You want to kill me now, yet I'm someone here to help you. The world around us is falling faster than you think. Now you are here, threatening someone who is here to try to survive because the REAL you is gone; you have been replaced with a soldier," he tells me.

"Y-you're… Shut up!" I stuttered out.

"I make a lot of sense," he says. "You know it."

"I-I said s-shut up!" I grip the gun with both hands. "I'll do whatever I have to to keep the people I love alive, even if it means killing you or dying." Right before I pull the trigger, his door bursts open and Allison is standing there.

"Put it down," she tells me.

"Stay out of this," I tell her.

"Miranda—" I cut her off.

"Leave or die, Jordan." I lower the gun. "You have until sundown to decide, or I will decide for you," I say and walk out, right past Allison.

"Miranda!" I hear Allison yell behind me, but I keep walking. "Miranda, stop!" She catches up to me and grabs my shoulder.

I stop in my tracks and turn around. "What," I say.

"What the hell were you thinking?" she asks. Great…here we go again.

"I know what I'm doing, so why don't you just stay out of it! This has nothing to do with you. I'm doing what is best for the group." I tell her. "Or what, do you still like him?" I ask.

"Miranda, are you serious?" she says. Yeah, I know I'm the crazy one.

"Look, I don't feel like talking about this. I told him what is gonna happen. I'm doing this for you guys and for me. We need this to happen. End of discussion." I walk away. This time cutting her off.

...Let's wait till nightfall...

I've been pacing back and forth in my room for a while now. Miko came in a little while ago and asked if I was hungry but I'm not. I can't believe Allison doesn't have my side in this! She is the one who didn't want him in the beginning and now all of a sudden she doesn't. THIS IS BULLSHIT! I punch my wall but it's so thick you can't hear anything, and I didn't even make a dent. Looking at my hand, though, you can see the bruise and slight swelling; it bruises so easily. I look out of my window and see the sun is starting to set. "Go time." I grab my gun from my bed and go to leave. But the door is locked from the outside. Fucking Allison must have done this to keep me from doing this. I start banging on the door really loud. "OPEN THE DAMN DOOR!" I yell and keep banging. You see, I would break it down, but I need it. "ALLISON, THIS ISN'T FUNNY!" I yell again and keep pounding the door, and no one is opening it. I'm like two seconds away from losing my shit completely.

"Can you stop banging so I can let you out," Allison says through the door.

"I swear to god if you don't unlock this door—" She cuts me off. *OH MY GOD.*

"You'll what? Hurt me? Or hurt the group?" she asks. Damn it...

"Just open it!" I kick the door.

"Fine!" She finally gives in. She unlocks the door, but before I can move she stops me. "Give me your gun." She holds out her hand.

"Hell no." I roll my eyes and push past her.

"Miranda!" she shouts.

I turn and look at her. "You're not stopping me," I say and run outside, and I see Jordan by the gate and the sun had set. "Yo, pretty boy, you leaving or what!" I shout.

"I'm not leaving." He turns to me.

"Wrong choice." I pull out my gun and aim right for his head, but—again!—this time Miko stands in front of it. "Really! You too!" I sigh, annoyed.

"Miranda, do you really wanna do this?" she asks me.

"Yes," I say coldly, still not moving.

"No, you don't," Allison says from behind me.

"What do you know!" I yell. "Maybe...maybe you should leave with him!" I say, immediately regretting that.

Everyone looks taken back from what I said. "Is...is that really...how do you feel?" I hear her stutter out. Greaaaat.

"I—" I look back at her still having the gun on Jordan, well, technically Miko.

"I don't wanna hear it... I can't do this with you." She shakes her head.

This time I lower my gun and completely turn and face her. "What's that supposed to mean...?" I ask, and she doesn't say anything. "Wow..." I trail off. We all are so quiet that you could hear a pin drop because no one dares to make a noise. I feel like everyone is just waiting for either one of us to explode. I can't believe this shit though; it's all his...no, my fault. It was still very quiet until...

"I'm so sorry," she says.

"Don't be, it's all my fault," I say, "but because I already fucked up." I throw my gun to the side and look at everyone. "You wanna stay?" I ask Jordan, and he nods.

"Then let's play Russian Roulette."

Everyone looks sorta pissed, but no one disagrees, and instead, we all take a seat. I can tell they don't wanna do this, but they really don't care at the same time. I guess it's time to prove Jordan right; we aren't people anymore. I sit down too, and the gun is in the center of us all; no one moves to grab it. "So, who wants to go first?" Jordan says.

"I'll go," I say and grab the gun from the middle. I point the gun to my head and glance around at everyone. For a moment it feels like time stands still, and even though everyone is staring at me, it feels like I am alone. Have you ever had those out-of-body experiences? It feels like I'm watching the gun to my head, and I'm screaming at myself to stop! To put it down. To make sure this doesn't get out of hand. But I still just watch. It's like my voice falls deaf onto my ears. I take a deep breath in and close my eyes. The gun clicked, but no bullet. I sigh a breath out and hand the gun to Allison.

She hesitantly takes the gun. "Here goes nothing..." she drags out, and puts the gun to her head. This time I almost didn't give it to her, but again, my body just doesn't listen to my mind. When I see the gun in her hand, my heart starts racing more than it did when it was in my own. What if the bullet is in the chamber? What if... I never get to apologize, make amends, or even hug her again. She pulls the trigger, but nothing again, she shakily hands the gun to Alex.

"Come on, guys, this is stupid," Miko says. "Alex, put it down." She tries to reach for the gun, but he snatches it back.

"It's fine." He puts the gun to his head and pulls it fast. Nothing. Alex has never been afraid of dying; he has come so close to death on numerous occasions. This is like second nature for him. I know he doesn't WANT to die, it's more he is ready for himself to die.

He hands it to Jordan. Jordan looks at all of us and then locks eyes with me almost like he is gonna point the gun at me, but instead, "Don't say I didn't warn you. We all die eventually." He puts the gun to his head and pulls the trigger.

He dropped to the floor, blood gushing from his head.

It was as if he knew the bullet was in the chamber, it was like he knew he would die. "Holy shit..." I trail out, even though I know this game. You never know how it really is until you experience it, and wow, is it not pretty. The scene right now was like an evil presence, other than the dead, has been lifted. I know it sounds horrible to admit, but even though Jordan was a good guy, he had a dark mask underneath. *We all do.*

"We should bury him with the others," Miko says... Is this girl serious?

"No," Alex says. Damn, first time he ever said no to her.

"What the hell did you just say to me?" Miko asks, shocked.

"I said no. This guy doesn't deserve our respect, compassion, and for damn sure shouldn't be buried with our friends," Alex snaps.

"He is still a human being." Miko points to Jordan's body. "And before you, before all of this, he was OUR friend." Miko then looks at me and Allison.

"Just because he was your friend in the past doesn't mean he was your friend now. He made OUR friend leave us. Fuck it, he made our two friends, whatever they had going on, split! He fought with us all consistently. That was not a human being, he was the dead…still breathing," Alex says.

"Now you're being ridiculous," Miko says.

Allison grabs my arm and whispers to me, "Shouldn't we break this up?"

"Just wait," I tell her.

"I'm the one that's being ridiculous?" Alex laughs.

"We. Are. Burying. Him," Miko tells Alex.

"No." Alex shrugs. Miko goes to make a move to the shovels, but Alex blocks her path "I'm serious," he says.

"Yeah, so am I." She tries to push past him, but he pushes her away. Alex doesn't know his own strength.

That's when Allison steps in. "Guys, come on." She goes in between them.

"Guys, you're fighting for no damn reason," I tell them. "If anything, fuck what we think. Allison should decide what happens to the body. He put her through worse these last couple of weeks, he made her have a nervous break, he made her leave, he just… It's her decision. Not ours," I say, and Allison just stares at me and mouths a "Really?" and I nod.

"You're right." Miko steps away.

Alex stands his ground. "I'm not gonna tell you what to do. But you know my opinion." He stands still by the shovels and graveyard, refusing to move a muscle.

"Why are you just standing there?" I ask.

"Because," he says with a sly smirk on his face.

Allison grabs my wrist and pulls me into the school and her room. She paces back and forth, refusing to stand still and look me in the eye. I can hear her mumbling things like "dead" and "human," but I can't make out much more. I don't wanna push her or speak up. I feel like it's best if I just let her relax because a lot must be going through her head right now thanks to me! After just pacing for about two minutes, she stops and looks me dead in the eyes. "Why did you say that?" she asks. You ever realize how living eyes could look dead? I'm starting to see that in ours.

"I said it because it's the truth," I tell her, and she sighs.

"I-I don't know what to do," she sighs out. "I mean, yeah, he did bad shit, but I don't know," she says.

"Now, don't look at me like I'm crazy but why don't you make a pros and cons list?" I suggest. At first…she looks at me like I was crazy. But then she starts thinking and nods to the idea. "I'll give you a thing he did: you say whether it is a good or bad thing and I tally it with…" I look around her room and find a pencil. "With this," I say.

She takes a shaky breath. "That isn't gonna help the situation. We aren't in school anymore, Miranda. This is someone's dead corpse we are talking about, not deciding on whether or not if we are gonna skip a class," she says.

"I'm just trying to help," I tell her. I know it may not be the best idea, but like, it's not like we have many options to do things.

"I know. Just give me a minute." She puts on a fake smile.

I grab both her hands. "Whatever you decide, I'll back you up. But you have to decide very soon because we can't just have a body laying around," I tell her, and she doesn't say anything, so I walk out. I go back outside and Alex and Miko are still arguing.

"Just because you wanna be cold hearted doesn't mean they have to listen to you," Miko says.

"Not everyone can be nice all the damn time to people! In case you forget, caring about everyone at this time gets you killed," Alex explains. He is talking about the time when these people needed "help," and because Allison and Miko are so nice, they offered to help, but the people came back and stole about eighty percent of our supplies. No, you can't trust anyone in this world either, but once we lose all trust, then we won't trust each other too.

"You are really getting me upset," Miko tells Alex.

"I'M getting YOU mad, really? You are gonna put us at risk," Alex says.

"Wow." Miko starts walking away.

"Don't walk away when we are talking." Alex grabs her wrist hard and pulls her back.

"Ow, Alex. Let go!" She tries to pull him off.

"Not until we are done," he says. This is way out of hand now. I know he gets angry and shit but don't put your hands on someone else. Even if it's just a grab.

"Alex, let her go!" I yell with my jaw clenched. Alex knows better than to put his hands on any of us.

"Okay," he says and lets her wrist go. You can see his handprint around her wrist. "I'm sorry, Miko. I didn't…" She puts her hand up.

"Just...ugh, leave me alone." She runs off into the school.

"We need to talk. Now," I tell him, and he just looks down like a kid who just took a cookie he wasn't supposed to. "What...the...fuck makes you think you could put your hands on her. You left a fucking mark!" I yell at him.

"I-I just uh," he stutters. He doesn't stutter at all. That's how you know he did something wrong. I don't know what came over me but hearing him not having anything to say enraged me more. I slap him hard across the right side of his face leaving a handprint. He stumbles back at first, then just grabs his face and looks at me, stunned.

"If you don't make this right, you're just like Jordan then," I tell him. "So this is what you're gonna do, you're going to apologize, make this right between you two. And if I EVER see you put your hands on Miko again, I don't care about our history, I'm kicking you out. Never put your hands on a girl!" I tell him.

"I won't, I promise. I-I wasn't thinking. But now I know my anger has gotten way too out of hand. I'll work on it from now on, I swear. Just please help me," he begs. Whenever he admits he is wrong he always sounds so sincere. I just hope he keeps it.

"I'll go talk to her for you," I tell him. I turn to go into the building, but Allison comes out, and I guess because she made a choice. "So, you decided?"

"We bury him with the others because he has done a lot of wrong but deserves a proper burial, everyone does," she says. "Alex, you're gonna help me. Miranda, go talk to Miko," she tells me, and we don't even put up any arguments. It was her choice, so I think Alex realizes we don't have to like it, but we have to accept it. "And after everything, Miranda, I would like to talk to you, please," she asks.

"Sure," I tell her, and run into the building. I knock on Miko's door softly and hear a faint "Come in," so I poke my head through the door and see her sitting on her bed with her eyes puffy like she has been crying. "Are you okay?" I come in and sit next to her. She shakes her head and cries into my shoulder. I let her cry for a little bit and rub her back. I hate seeing them cry, but when they cry, I get all awkward and don't know what to do for anyone, so I just wait and try to be as less awkward as possible. Especially with Miko. She never really cries, so when she does I definitely don't know what to do. "What is bothering you so much? Is it because of Alex?" I ask.

"Yes, but not for the reason you think. Even though he never put his hands on me, the mark is just about gone." She shows me her wrist, and she was right, it was only a little pinkish.

"What's wrong, then?" I ask, and she wipes her tears and looks at me seriously.

"Whatever I tell you. You can't tell him. At all. Promise me," she says.

"I promise," I tell her.

"I-I… My period is um, l-late," she stutters out.

"So…" I trail off.

"I think I may be pregnant, okay!" she blurts out, and I don't say anything. "Say something, please" She starts to tear up again.

"No, no, no, don't cry. I don't know what to say because I wanna make a joke but at the same time be serious," I say.

"Tell me both," she suggested.

"Okay, don't get mad, then," I say. "Serious note, you might not be. Joke… OUUUUU cherry popped!" She slaps my arm. "You said I could!" I laugh.

"You're…an ass," she says.

"You cursed. Holy Jesus, only took you to the apocalypse to start cursing." I laugh even more.

"God, I wish I never told you." She rolls her eyes and places her head in her hands.

"Aw, come on. You don't even know it for sure," I tell her.

"I know but that doesn't make it anymore nerve racking and scary," she says.

She looks so worried. We never talked about if one of us got pregnant or anything like that. I mean I bet it is bound to eventually happen, but, like, now that it could actually happening, it is kind of exciting yet very terrifying. I pull her into a hug. "We are gonna be fine, and after all, I'm sure if there is a baby in there, then they will be fine too, and if no baby, then life continues on." I rub her arm.

Allison comes in and sees Miko upset. "Is everything okay?" she asks.

"Yeah it's jus—" Miko cuts me off… You know, I can't stand speaking anymore.

"Yep! Everything is fine," she jumps in. Why doesn't she want Allison to know? But Allison told me to check on her. I guess she just knew she was upset.

"Uh…okay." Allison looks between us and shrugs.

"I know what we need. Why don't we kick Alex to his original room and we all hang out in here tonight," I suggest.

"That…that doesn't sound so bad," Miko says.

"I'll go tell him to sleep in his room," I say. I get up and go outside. When I go out, I see Alex standing by what I'm assuming is Jordan's grave, just staring at it. "Uhhh, dude?" I say, and he snaps back into reality.

"Oh shit, I'm sorry… Just thinking," he tells me.

"Okay then? Just came to tell you to sleep in your room tonight," I tell him.

"Wait, why?" he asks.

"Miko isn't feeling the best, so me and Allison are gonna spend time with her," I explain. "Hypothetically, of course, do you think if one of us had a kid it would be good for the group?" There is always a chance, right? Just should get his general idea.

He looked taken aback at the sudden question. "I mean…at the end of the day if we were all here to support, take care, and love the child, then I wouldn't mind. Because if you think about it, kids are very hard to raise in general, so can you imagine now? Not trying to rant or anything but yeah… a kid would be nice," he finishes. Well, at least I know if she is pregnant, he is fine with it.

"Okay, well, I'm gonna get back to the girls." I start to walk off, but he grabs me by my wrist.

"Wait," he says.

"Uh, what, Alex?" I ask.

"You have my back no matter what, right? Like at the end of the day you won't have anything bad happen to me? Even if Miko and Allison say otherwise? Please. It's important," he asks. He sounds scared when he is talking, like he did something.

"What did you do?" I ask, and yank my wrist back.

"Nothing… I just want to know," he says.

"I'll have your back, Alex. Right or wrong, we stick it out till the end.

But if something goes too far south, I'm not sure. I can't say I will ALWAYS have your back because it does depend on the situation and what has happened. And if you got Allison and Miko upset over the things that you had done, then it would be pretty hard to have your back unless I no doubt agree with why or what you did. I'm sorry if that didn't give you any clarification or anything but it is my honest answer," I tell him.

"Yeah, I guess that makes sense. I didn't do anything, I swear. I just would like to feel a little sense of security or loyalty. Not saying that you guys don't, but it's like, I know I fuck up a lot and I can sometimes be a dick, but just know that whatever I do is the best for the group. I'm not saying it is right but in my dumbass brain it might be, but I'll always put you guys first," he says. Where is all this coming from?

"Okay, Alex." I patted his shoulder. "Get some sleep," I tell him and walk off. Why the hell is he acting so weird? I thought it was weird asking him about the potential of a baby coming, and he wants to talk about his loyalty to the group? Maybe he is just being more unstable than usual. We definitely need to keep a better eye on him and make sure he feels better. I stand at the end of the hall and sigh. "I don't think he would do anything," I whisper and rub my head with my hand. We don't need any more drama! I'm getting tired of this, I'm tired of all of this. I don't think I could handle another loss, especially one of us who are left.

Allison comes out from the room. "Hey, I was wondering what was taking you so long. Uh, what's wrong?" she asks. Yeah, like I wanna tell her.

"Nothing, don't worry," I tell her. We just stand there in awkward silence. Of course it's awkward to just stand around your sorta ex yet also your sorta co-leader.

"We should go back inside." She points to the door.

"You said you wanted to talk to me… After the burial," I reminded her.

"Oh yeah, it's nothing," Allison says. *Obviously it is something.* We go inside and sit with Miko.

"So, what now?" I ask.

"We play a game!" Miko suggests. "It hasn't always worked out in the past, but we are pretty much always most civil out of the group unless you count Uno. But let's not and play something like 'would you rather,'" she says.

"Sure," I say, and Allison nods. "I'll go first. Would you rather have feet like bigfoot or eyes the size of bowling balls?" I laugh at my own question. *God, you would never think I'm like nineteen.*

"Definitely bigfoot feet," Miko says.

"Uh, bowling balls for eyes," Allison says.

"What? Why?" Miko says.

"So I can see everything." Allison laughs.

"I would have to agree with Miko on this one… I already have big-ass feet," I comment, and we all laugh this time.

"Okay, my turn! Would you rather be able to pause or rewind time?" Miko asks.

"Rewind," Allison and I say at the same time. God, if I could rewind I would change so much that has happened to us as a group. Kev dying, all the arguments, Allison and my break-up, but I wouldn't change this from happening. It sounds weird because, obviously, I don't like what is happening and, obviously, I hate that we are in this predicament, but this helped us in a way too. Like if I really think about it, if it wasn't for this apocalypse, I wouldn't spend so much time with my friends, I wouldn't have gotten out of some really tough situations, and as weird as it sounds, I feel like I have more freedom now than I ever did. Before this happened, we were all about sixteen, still living at home and miserable, but now we are on our own, and yeah, it's hard, but we have the freedom to live. I know we all lost so many friends and family members along the way, and we don't have a chance to "follow our dreams," but we have each other. That's all that matters.

"If I could rewind, I would stop this whole thing from happening," Allison says.

"Uh…yeah, me too," I say. They would think I'm crazy if I told them what I just thought.

"Really, Miranda? I would think you would want to rewind to before you guys bro—" I cut Miko off.

"Allison, it's your turn!" I say. I'm trying to FORGET those feelings.

"Right. Would you rather have tattoos or piercings?" she says.

"Tattoos," I say. Let's ignore the fact I have earrings and a nose ring, shall we?

"Yeah, tattoos," Miko agrees.

"Let's do something else, guys" I say.

"We should probably get to sleep," Miko says. "It's getting late."

"You're right." I yawn. We say our goodnights. Allison and I agreed that her and Miko could share the bed and I would sleep on the floor with a pillow and blanket.

Tonight, I couldn't sleep. I'm used to this, though. Usually, I wouldn't sleep for sometimes nights at a time until my body finally crashes. I know it isn't exactly healthy, but sleeping has always been a struggle, so I really don't care. I'm pretty sure Alex is taking the lookout shift right now because we are all here and stuff. Maybe I should check? No, I don't wanna wake them. Everything seems so long ago now. Like those people trying to invade us feels like ancient history. I should try to sleep. I close my eyes, and my body starts aching, so I start tossing and turning, but nothing is helping. Probably because I'm on the fucking hard, cold floor. I sneeze and sit up with my back on the wall. Yeah no, I think I'm getting sick. "Hey, Miranda. Are you okay?" Miko whispers.

"Sorry, I didn't mean to wake you," I whisper back.

She gets out of bed quietly and sits next to me. "You didn't wake me now, I heard you tossing and turning." She laughs quietly.

I cover my mouth and stifle a cough. "Haha, yeah." I half smile.

"Are you feeling okay?" she asks.

"I think I'm getting sick, but don't worry, it doesn't matter," I brush it off. "Alex and I need to go out hunting, so I can't let this cough get in the way," I say.

She places her hand on my forehead and then my neck. "You're a little hot," she says.

"Miko, I'm flattered but—" I laugh, and she slaps me slightly on the back of the head. "Ow, you know I was joking." I laugh. "Well, let's hope that clears up," I say.

"Do you wanna sleep…in your bed?" she asks.

"No, I'm fine," I say.

"I don't feel so good myself," she says.

"Take it easy tomorrow, no training, no lookout, no anything," I tell her.

"Okay, let's try to sleep again," she says, and gets back into her bed.

"I'll try," I say and lie back down.

*   *   *

Why couldn't all sickness go away? I wake up with a pounding headache and feeling way worse than I felt last night. My nose is running, my stomach feels queasy, and my throat is killing me. I sigh and lie back down because it doesn't look like I can do anything. No, I have to. I stand up and feel a little lightheaded. I look to the bed, and the girls aren't there. "Guess they didn't want to bother me," I say to myself and go outside and sit down at the table.

"Morning," Allison says. I just give a half-ass wave and put my head down.

Alex comes up behind me and places his hand on the table. "We should head out after breakfast." I give him a thumbs up. My stomach is definitely not up to eating right now, but I guess I could try.

I try to take a bite of the bread and immediately regret it and gag. "I-I'm not…" I clear my throat. "I'm not hungry," I say and push the food away.

"Come on, Miranda, eat something, please," Allison says.

"I don't want to," I say.

"Please, for me?" she says. That isn't fair… I'm sick!

"Ugh, I'll try," I cough out, and take another bite of the bread, but my stomach is still doing flips and turning. It's like a roller coaster and one of those spin rides put together. "Yeah, never mind." I push the food away again.

Allison puts her hand on my back. "Are you okay?" she asks, concerned.

"Yeah, just a little under the weather," I tell her. More like a lot under the weather, it's like a storm, but let's keep that to myself.

She rubs my back. "Well, if you want, I'll go hunting with Alex today," she says. She's always trying to be protective.

"No, I'm fine," I say.

"No she isn't," Miko chimes in. This girl is like a ninja! "She didn't sleep much, and had a slight fever," she says.

"That's it, you're not going," Allison says.

"But…come o—" I cut my own sentence short by coughing.

"I already said no." Allison gets up. "Alex! It's me and you today."

"Sure," he says.

"I want to go!" I whine.

"You have to get better, Miranda," Alex says. "I need you right now." He hugs me and then whispers in my ear, "You need to be ready for anything."

Before I could react, "Alex, let's go, shit," Allison says, and they take off.

I put my head back down on the table. "I'm gonna make you some soup," Miko says. Maybe it was a good thing I didn't go today. I mean, I am sick. But that shouldn't slow us down or anything. I don't like having a personal struggle. It's stupid and unnecessary because it shows you're weak and a liability. I wonder if maybe I can convince Miko to allow me to at least go to the river and help them fish after soup. Right now they are probably scouting, then hunting, then fishing, and, usually, but not now since Allison went hunting, someone tends to the garden, but Miko is probably gonna do that today. We don't have many lookouts anymore; we just have been trying to focus on the group's dynamic and our relationships. Alex is the main lookout now; he does it at night since he is a "night owl" even though I tell him all the time I don't mind. He lets me do it every few days when he wants extra time with Miko. During the day there is no one since we can see through the school's gate, but after dinner that's it. I don't do training anymore; it isn't like I need to anyway, since I'm always out living what we are training. Miko still trains almost every other day because she doesn't hunt much, not by her choice, she is actually really good, but I think Allison and I just do it without thinking, but then again, Miko never puts up a fight. I think she prefers cooking and just being inside, then again, I'm not sure. Allison… She's kind of an everyday person, like her chores later, she has her main garden, but other than that she can pretty much do anything, so she is probably the easiest since she just says what she wants and does it. Alex is always a hunter; he loves the adrenaline, the killing, and the experience, or so he says. Can't say I blame him. It can be cool yet scary at the same time. It's probably only scary because we have people we need to protect, and without us, something might fall through; one of them might get hurt or even die. So the pressure is like, a hundred times higher than if you are alone.

"Miranda!" Miko yells and places the bowl down. "You all right?" she asks.

"Yeah…just thinking. Probably a little too much because now my head hurts." I laugh, and start eating the soup. "How about you?" I ask.

"Well, when I woke up today, I felt really nauseous, so that's not a good sign." She sighs and looks down.

"Having a baby isn't a bad thing, Miko. We need some sort of joy and sunshine, otherwise we get swallowed up by the dark and depression. It's already happening to us. If you really are pregnant, don't think of it as a burden, think about it as a blessing," I told her, but she doesn't say anything. "I'm gonna go down by the river," I tell her.

"No," she says.

"Yes, right after soup!" I say and eat.

"You really shouldn't go," she tries to warn me, but I just keep eating. "I know you are trying to eat fast so you can go." I give a sly smirk and just keep eating again. "I know you think it's just a cough, but it can turn into more if you don't take care of it," she says.

I finished up the last of the soup. "All done, now I will be back." Before she could rebuttal, I ran out of the school.

We make our own rules

As I'm running to the river, I hear faint cries for help coming from the river, almost like a cry for help but so quiet that it sounds like an infant as well. I run a little faster, and I stop dead in my tracks. Allison is nowhere in sight. I'm guessing she's in shed-looking thingy that, of course, is surrounded by like, six zombies, and I see Alex trying to fight one off him because his gun is on the floor. THIS IS WHY WE USE TWO WEAPONS, PEOPLE! *But either way there aren't many around this area…* it looks like they ran into this little swarm of them and everything just went south. I see Alex start losing the fight, so without hesitation I pull out my dagger while running up to Alex and I stab the zombie through its head and it drops to the floor. Alex bends over, panting. "You just saved my ass," he breathes out and picks up his gun.

"Well, we aren't done yet," I say, pointing to the shed. He aims his gun too start shooting, but I grab it and push it down. "Too much noise. We already see some, we don't need anymore," I whisper. We both scan around looking for anything that could be used as a weapon, and he spots a jagged piece of glass and picks it up.

"Good enough," he says.

"Now let's save her," I say. We take out the first two pretty easy, just stabbing them in the back of their heads. I throw the one I just killed to another one and kick it in its leg so it falls and I stomp its head into the ground. "Fuck, my shoes," I whisper and just shrug it off. The last one I stab it through its eye; that's the last one to fall.

"Allison, it's me, Alex. Miranda is with me," he says, but we don't get an answer….

"Fuck it," I say and kick the door, one, twice, and a third time, making it come of the hinges. "Allison!" I shout and run over to her. "Are you okay?" I ask.

"Yeah, no bites," she says. It looks like two more were in here and she had to get them but I'm gonna take a wild guess and say it was hard.

"We have to stop almost dying around each other," I say and put on a half-smile.

"Yeah we do." She laughs lightly.

"Although this is cute, we still need food and to get back to my girlfriend," Alex says.

"What did you guys find?" I ask.

Allison opens a bag and pulls out a can of beans and a rabbit. "This will do for tonight and tomorrow. If some of the vegetables are done we can have a soup or something small for tomorrow," she says.

"Some are. Miko made me some soup earlier," I say.

"Well, then it's perfect. Oh and we also found a bottle of oxy and something for sleeping. There isn't much left in either, so I'm guessing no one saw the need for sleeping meds, and oxy only has like five left so maybe they thought they took them all but didn't," Allison says.

"Let's just hope more people aren't back," I say. I much rather deal with zombies than fully capable people.

"Let's not wait around to find out," Alex says and starts leaving. What stick is up his ass?

I go to start walking but Allison stops me, "Wait," she says. We wait a few seconds. "Miko, you, and me have to have a talk probably in the next couple of days," she says.

"What did he do?" I ask.

"Don't worry about it now," she brushes it off.

"Okay, let's catch up with him before he leaves for good," I say. I hold my hand out and she takes it without even questioning it, and we both had a faint smile on our faces while we go catch up with Alex. The whole walk home I couldn't help but think about three specific things: Miko being nauseous, what just happened and what might happen, and Alex. Miko's thing is still not confirmed but is still something to think about. What just happened has been happening too much. Allison and I have to have a talk about that one-on-one and then with the group. We can't afford to lose anybody else, and not only that, these things could easily be avoided if simple steps were followed. With Alex I think— No, I KNOW he is planning something in his head about something he wants to do, the only huge question is, will he go through with it or just have his thoughts stay a thought?

"What are you thinking about?" Allison asks.

"Nothing," I say.

"Bullshit," she says.

"Just that me and you have to talk before Miko, you, and me talk. We need to talk about our group and next steps," I tell her.

"I agree," she says.

"Now we just see what happens," I say

"Isn't that all you can do?" Alex looks back.

"It really is," Allison says.

We arrive at the entrance of the school. "Before we go in, what happened to you guys?" I ask.

"Well, we were walking to the river, and we heard the gurgling noises, but we thought it was behind us. We ran, but we ran right into them. We did the best we could 'cause there was like ten, maybe twelve. Allison thought it would be a good idea to hide out in the shed, but when I turned she was already gone, so I was gonna try to get there, but one came up behind me, and well, that's when you showed up," Alex explains.

"I'm just glad I showed up." I sigh.

"Me too," they both say at the same time.

When we arrive at the school, Miko runs and hugs us all. "You guys were taking so long. I got so worried," she says.

"We sorta got attacked," Allison says.

"We're okay now," Alex reassures.

"Yeah, because Miranda saved our asses," Allison says. I side-hug her and laugh.

"Without her help I would be dead," Alex says.

We can see the look of shock and fear on Miko's face. "I'm glad I didn't stop you," she says.

She is right. If she would have stopped me we would have lost Alex and most likely Allison too. I know our group is just a bunch of teens, but we try our best and do our best. This is now a world where we are set up to die and lose, yet we are alive. "Miko, I need to talk to you." Alex pulls Miko to the side, and Allison and I go up to the lookout area.

"I feel like it's been years since we have been up here." She sighs.

"Yeah," I say. She wasn't wrong. Alex and she have both been REFUSING to let me do night watches anymore, since I would stay up all night, but now it's Alex, but I'm sure he sleeps on the job too; he is just a light sleeper. For me, yeah, the slightest thing wakes me up, but when I'm tired it's harder.

We stare out. The sun is starting to set. "I wish I still had a camera," Allison says sadly.

"Why would you want to capture this world?" I ask.

"I know it's evil and, well, dead, but still, look at that sunset! Small things in this world that we used to take for granted are still around and we can enjoy them. I guess it's kind of stupid but I wish I could capture them because…" She trails off as if she didn't like her thought.

"Because it isn't promised for us tomorrow," I finish her sentence. *We always understand each other's thoughts.*

"What's one thing you wish you had back?" she asks me.

"Honestly? I wish I still had my old papers of songs, scripts, stories, and poems," I tell her. I used to love writing for expression, but I wanted to travel around the world as a job. I don't exactly know how, but just a chance to go anywhere. I always wanted to go exploring.

"I remember those." She puts a faint smile on.

I look around the lookout spot. Fuck, not here. Must be in my room. "You know, I have paper and some colored pencils if you want," I tell her. I know she knows because sneaking into my room to get them is how she wrote her goodbye note.

"Yeah, I know. I don't want any yet. I have an idea," she says. "Come on," she gestures, and we climb down. Alex and Miko seem to be having a really deep conversation, not an argument but intense.

"We should let them be," I say. Right as I say that, Alex and she finish, because of course! (Doesn't even surprise me anymore.)

They both go their separate ways. Miko goes to cook and Alex to his room. Allison leans over "I can't tell if they are mad or not," she whispers.

"Me either." I shrug. It doesn't look like they are mad, they look hurt… No, hurt isn't the right word; they look lost. "I'll go talk to Alex and you talk to Miko," I say, and we split up. I run into the dorm and open Alex's door to see him just sitting there staring at the ceiling. "Hey" I say.

"Hey, Miranda." He sits up. "You can close the door," he says. I close the door behind me and sit next to him. Obviously, Alex and me…we are kind of just what we are. Like we were close friends; I knew he always had my back. He wasn't— isn't perfect, but still, we all know me and him had "a thing," but it's gone. It ended when the world ended, but I know I can still count on him, and plus he makes a better couple with Miko. They are total opposites, and I think that's why I think they look well.

"Are you and Miko okay?" I ask.

"Yeah, we kind of just both asked each other really shocking question. I asked her about my mistakes and what would be her breaking point, and she asked about babies," he says.

"Oh, okay. I got nervous there for a second. We don't need any more break ups," I say.

"Wait a sec, you two aren't back together?" he asks.

"No, why?" I say.

"I just thought you guys patched it up. I wouldn't think a stupid little thing like the Jordan situation would really end you guys for good," he says; he was right.

"It's just complicated I guess." I shrug.

He pulls me into a hug. "We are gonna get through this as a group; we got each other. I got you," he says.

I hug him back. "I know," I breathe out and pull away.

Allison is so right about things we take for granted. Before this all happened, we ignored the sunsets, ignored the peacefulness, never took the time to just breathe and just be with each other in a moment. No one really stopped to relax, no one stopped to think, and no one thought positive. Now we can breathe, now we can stop and take time to relax, take time to see the sunset, and take time to just be in the moment, not thinking ahead to get to your next destination. It shows you that the world was going to shit anyway; one way or another, humanity always fucks it up. Miko comes in. "Dinner is ready, guys," she says.

"Actually, I'm not that hungry, still feeling a little queasy." I stand up. "I'm going to bed early," I say.

"Are you sure?" Miko ask.

"Yeah. Goodnight, people. Tell Allison I said goodnight," I say and go to my room. I look under the bed and pull out the paper and colored pencils. God, I wish I had a pen instead. I sit on the floor and just hover the pencil over the paper. I glance over and see the picture of the beach I drew, but I look over again and see the picture of the sunset I drew during the watches. I don't know why but drawing just seems the most peaceful now, because writing is expressing emotions and just going with it, and drawing, well… for me…is capturing the moment. *It's my version of a camera.* But today, Allison and my three-minute conversation made me want to try again. I used to write a lot when this first started, just trying to remember everything and just say what's happening. I still have them with my old photos. I figured maybe someone would find them one day and realize that there were people trying and living in this mess. Should I write a story? A poem? Or something else? "Poem," I whisper, and put the pencil to the paper…

Title - Human?
By Miranda
We should come together during a time of need
Love, support, and cherish each other.
Instead we laugh or ignore when people bleed
We lost everyone, sisters… Maybe a brother.
"Ugh, think, stupid brain! Just like the old days"
We should be fighting the creatures
And saving the humans.
Instead we aren't looking for cures
"This is a stretch."
No one knows how much danger we are in.
We aren't human anymore
We all have monsters within

"No," I say and crumple the paper and throw it to the side and pull out another one. "Maybe…. Maybe… ugh, nevermind," I say and push the stuff back under the bed. I get into my bed and stare at the wall on my side. I know what I can do! Why the hell didn't I think of this before! I grab a knife and carve my name and three quotes into the wall.

"We got each other."

"Fight, fight for everything you want."

And, "We'll be okay."

These are the quotes always circling my mind. I rub my hand over the wall and close my eyes to let out a shaky breath. I hope they are true because then we shouldn't be fighting anymore. I know that we all think it would be easier to just give up, but there has to be a reason that we keep going. It's hope, it's so stupid but true. I look out the window and see Alex pacing as if he is trying to determine something, but I look away anyway. "Maybe I should sleep," I say and lie down and close my eyes. UPDATE: didn't sleep.

I'm the first to "wake up," so I go outside and tell Alex he can come down and we both sit down. "You look like hell," he says.

"Yeah, I feel like it too." I laugh.

"It's so early. You just missed the sunrise," he says. Damn, I can't tell if the sunrise or the sunset is better.

"Wanna spare?" I ask.

"Awww hell yeah!" he says and jumps up. I get up too and we move to the side.

"Remember, we aren't trying to break anything for the other person. First person to tap out or bleed, even if it's the slightest, then we done," I go over the rules, and he nods. We both put up our fists. I'm the first to throw a punch, but it was a fake one. He goes to block that one, so I swing and punch him in his side.

"Nice," he says. This time he tries to swing, but I lock and twist his arm behind his back. Alex and I have always been best fighters, not because of how fast we think about the next punch but our reflexes; we all have good reflexes. Right now I have his arm behind his back, he swings his leg over and drops is both to the ground, and I land on my elbow, but I get up fast and he gets up right after me.

"Slow ass," I joke, and he rolls his eyes. We didn't even notice Allison and Miko were watching us. We were just consumed into the "fight." We aren't allowed to punch each other in the face either. It's all neck and lower, even though he prefers no one hits in between his legs. I guess I was too busy in thought, so he uses it as an advantage and kicks my leg out from behind me so I fall on my face. "Fuck!" I say, not that it hurt, but I feel blood dripping from my nose. I guess I fell hard.

He quickly helps me up. "Oh my god, I'm so sorry." He looks at my nose.

"It's fine. It didn't even hurt." I squeeze my nose and hold my head back.

"Miranda, are you okay!" Allison and Miko run over.

"Yeah, fell the wrong way. Was a good spare though." I high-five Alex.

"Come, I'll help you get in cleaned," Allison says and drags me to the "nurse's office," a.k.a. where we hold the medicine. She pulls out a rag and dabs around my nose and holds it in place.

"You know I'm not five, right?" I say.

"I know. I just want to make sure it is cleaned right. You have some small cuts around it. We should clean it," she says and grabs the peroxide

"NO! Get that peroxide the hell away from me!" I say and move back…. Okay, so maybe I am five-year-old in a teenage body.

"Miranda, we don't need it getting infected," she says, slightly annoyed but mostly worried.

"Tiny cuts hurt more!" I shout.

"But it's over quicker," she tells me.

"It doesn't even hurt," I say, annoyed.

"I don't care." Allison shrugs.

"B-but it's…it—" I hate disinfecting. I don't care how tough I am; this is one of the rare pain things I can't handle.

"It's only gonna sting a little, you can squeeze my hand while I do it." She holds my hand. "Close your eyes," Allison says, and I take a deep breath and close my eyes tightly.

She dabs the cuts, and I hiss and squeeze her hand slightly. When she pulls the rag away, I breathe out. "You done?" I ask and open my eyes.

"Yes, it wasn't that bad," she says with a big-ass evil grin.

"You know I hate that." I roll my eyes.

Miko comes in. *Damn, this girl is everywhere.* "Hey um," She hesitates, then breaks into a smile. "Do we still have pads?" She jumps up and down slightly.

"Aww no baby!" I say sadly.

"Nope!" She claps. Allison hands her a pad. "Don't get me wrong, I was thinking about how the baby would bring so much happiness, but it's best for right now we all wait," she explains.

"I wanted to be an aunt," I whine.

"Soon, but not today," she says, "Anyway, Miranda, how is your nose?" she asks.

"It's fine, even disinfecting it—" Allison cut me off.... *I don't care anymore!*

"She flinched and acted like a baby," she says.

"Pfffft did not," I say.

"Yeahhhh totally," Allison says, and we both start laughing.

"Can you guys leave for a second?" Miko says, so we leave. Today is a lazy day. No one wants to go out because of yesterday. I'm injured, and now Miko is on her period, so we basically have nothing to do. Unless I suggest we play a game? Nahhhh. Miko comes back out. "Guys, let's do something! I'm bored as hell. Let's play a game," she says.

"Okay, babe," Alex says, and I make a fake gagging noise. Allison slaps my shoulder slightly.

"Why don't we play two truths and one lie," I suggest.

"What are we...ten?" Allison says.

"Yes," all three of us say at the same time.

"Can't argue with that," she says.

"Miko goes first," I say, and everyone agrees, and she just side-eyes me.

"Okay. I hated math in school, I can't swim, and I never did anything illegal," she finishes. This one is sorta tough, but I think I know. "Miranda, what do you say?"

"You can't swim?" I say.

"Allison," Miko points.

"I agree with Miranda."

"Alex?" she says.

"You never did anything illegal." Alex laughs.

"Well, the lie is...that I can't swim," she says.

Allison and I high-five each other and Alex just huffs. "I'll go next," I say and laugh. "Okay, I used to play basketball, I hate listening to music, and I was supposed to go to college early." This should be very easy for all of them.

"Hated music."

"That you hated music."

"I know you loved music so the second one."

I nod. "Yep, all three of you are right. Good job." I high-five all of them.

"Let's eat!" Alex says. Miko goes to check the food and serve us all. Today we are having rabbit and soup. It's actually not that bad, but then again, we are in a life-or-death situation. I'm pretty sure we would be happy to eat anything.

"So I was thinking and, Miko, why don't you come hunting with me tomorrow?" I ask.

"Really? I would love to. I need to get out of here." She sighs dramatically, and we all laugh.

"I don't want her going," Alex says.

"Why?" Miko asks.

"Because it's dangerous. You know what happened to Allison and me just the other day. Why would I want you to go out there?" he tells her.

"Look around you, Alex. In case you forgot but all around us is dangerous. I know how to hold a gun, a bow and arrow, and I'm old enough to make my own damn decisions so I'm going with Miranda," Miko says. Great… I think this girl is about to explode too.

"Guys, come on, no fighting at the table," Allison says. "Alex, Miko wants to go so she is gonna go and that is final. Now let's stop with the pointless bickering." Allison points at both of them.

"I'm sorry." Miko sinks in her seat slightly.

But Alex looks out of thought, so I snap my fingers in front of his face. "Oh yeah, sorry," he mumbles and continues eating.

Once we are done, everyone goes in their own direction. I go to the graveyard. I haven't been there in a few days. I ran my fingers across each person's name slowly and thought about some of the last thing I remember clearly—

*Kevin: "I'll be okay…" *Bang**

"I miss you so much, Kev."

Victoria: *I see Victoria roll her eyes. "What now? I thought today was our day off!"*

"You never did wanna work, Victoria. I couldn't believe who you became."

Justin: *"Allison, stop!" Justin yells while trying to pull Allison off Victoria, but Allison stabs him in his chest.*

"Rest in peace, Justin. You didn't deserve this."

Jordan: "Let's play Russian Roulette."

"I know you had your own demons and tried to have a good heart, but you tried to tear my group apart. I hope you're burning in hell." I rub my hands together. Every time I visit these, memories come back, not the good memories from school but the memories of death, anger, and sadness. This just what the world has become. There is no before, there shouldn't be any history, it's only now pain and lost. Hey, at least we are still going, right? At least we are becoming stronger? I'm not sure what to say to be honest. I just know one day at a time…. Just…one…day…at…a…time. We must be patient with each other. It looks like everyone is on edge, about to snap and about to go like, kill each other again. I know it's not easy, but we have to remember again that we are all we have left in this world. They don't see that, and I need to make them see that. So many things have tried so many times to rip this group apart, but no one and nothing can. We are too strong and care too much to let that happen. So we will keep fighting, even if it kills us.

They are worth dying for….

I ended up falling asleep against the wall outside. "Hey, Miranda," Allison whispers and shakes my knee slightly.

I open my eyes and groan. "My neck." I rub my neck and get up.

"They aren't talking to each other. They started arguing in Miko's room last night, so I had to remove him. I think they were arguing about decisions, yet we are in charge." She laughs slightly. "Nevertheless, we have work to do, so let's go to it." She claps her hands together.

"Hey— Never mind." I was about to ask a dumb question. We go to sit down at the table and the anger in the open space is suffocating. I grab an apple.

"I'm still going with you, Miranda," Miko says.

"Ugh! Why don't you ever listen!" Alex yells.

"Because you're not my father, you're my boyfriend, and I know how to take care of myself," Miko snaps back.

"I'm so sorry that I'm scared of losing you," Alex says.

"You never listen to me, what is the big deal!" Miko sighs, annoyed.

"How do you go from almost never going out to going out? That makes no sense." Alex stands up.

"I'm trained." Miko starts tapping the table furiously.

"Not as well trained as I am," Alex says.

Miko almost completely slams her hands down. "I'm so sick of people thinking I'm weak or untrained or not good enough. I know how to shoot more than one weapon and how to use and do way more than you could ever do. I can do whatever the hell I want, that's what makes this my life and not yours. So stop acting like my goddamn dad and start acting like my boyfriend. And oh yeah, one more thing, don't you EVER underestimate me again." I have never ever seen Miko this mad before. I mean, yeah, I have seen her annoyed or mad but never like this. It's about time; her voice needs to be heard more and she needs to be like this more often. I always knew she has a badass side. *Okay, my bi is showing,* I laugh at myself. Then I hear a noise.

"Guys…" I trail off, looking at the gate.

"You are such an insensitive prick!" Miko yells.

"Well, you're nothing but a—" I cut Alex off.

"Guys!" I shout, and both of them freeze and see that like, twenty-five zombies are approaching the school gate. "I'll get up to the lookout spot, you guys fight what you can off," I tell them and run off. I basically jump up the ladder and pull out my gun and start shooting, but some still make it past the gate.

One down, then two, then three, then I just hit my fourth one when I heard, "Miranda, help!" I'm not exactly sure who called me, but I look down and see Miko getting cornered, Alex fighting, and Allison is nowhere to be seen. I jump down. There are only about thirteen left. Do I go for Miko? Or go look for Allison? "Miranda, find Allison! I got Miko!" Alex starts running into a big group of them, and I stand there, looking around.

I feel something grab my shoulder. I turn around and shoot it in the head. "Fuck that was…close." I breathe out and stab another one through the head.

"Miranda! They are both here!" Alex shouts, and I run to him. I see the girls struggling to keep them off. "We have to save them," he says.

"Then stop talking and do something!" I yell and start shooting, I only have four bullets left and the rest of my bullets are in my room. There are still eight left, so I shoot four down, and Alex kills the other four. We all sigh a breath of relief and group hug. That was a close call…too close.

We pull separate, and Allison hugs me separate, then the group hugs. "I thought I was done," she whispers.

"But you're alive, I got you." I rub her back.

"This is exactly why I don't want you going out," Alex says. At first Miko doesn't say anything, but I notice her fists clench. "Did you hear me?" Alex asks. This time Miko snaps. "Shut up! I swear to fucking god!" Everyone just stands there in shock. I've never seen Miko so angry.

"I'm just—" Alex tries to interrupt.

"No, you're gonna listen to me!" Miko yells. "I'm so sick and tired of people trying to underestimate me! You're supposed to support me, not act like you're my damn father!" She punches him in his shoulder. He reacts and grabs both her wrist tightly.

I grab Alex, Allison grabs Miko, and we pull both of them apart. "You guys seriously need to chill the fuck out!" I yell.

"I said he is gonna listen to me," Miko says.

Alex grabs her shoulder. "Let's talk." He pushes her to the side.

"You think you should follow them?" Allison says.

"Uhhh, why me?" I ask.

"'Cause I said so." She smiles fake evilly.

"Okay." I roll my eyes. I go up to them and watch in hearing distance to catch what they're saying.

"Why do you always do this?" I hear Miko say.

"In case you forgot, you just almost died, and well, I don't know, I just saved you!" Alex says.

"Miranda helped you too," Miko says.

"Exactly, you had to be saved. You can't save yourself." Alex sighs.

"You have no idea what I can do." Miko folds her arms.

"I know more than you think," Alex says.

Miko steps closer. "Do you? Do you really? Because I don't think so." She pokes his chest. "'Cause if you did you would know that I have killed before." Another jab to the chest. "I know how to work a gun." Grab number three. "And I'm not a little kid!" She pushes him.

"Stop putting your hands on me," he says, pushing her away. He pushed her too hard, so she ended up banging her back against the wall. "You aren't as strong as me or Miranda. What don't you understand!" Alex yells.

"No...I do. I understand...clearly" Miko breathes out. She turns around and I see her pull out a knife.

"I'm sorry for pushing you..." Alex stands up and holds his arm out. Miko turns around and stabs Alex in his arm and drags the knife down. "Ahhh fuck!" He pushes her away again and drops to his knees.

"I'm tired of people underestimating me," Miko says.

I run to him. "Oh shit, Alex." I grab his wrist and see the deep stab wound and the long gash going from right after his elbow to right before his wrist. "Go to Allison now. See if she can stitch you up. Hurry!" I tell him, and he nods, gripping his arm as he runs away. I sigh and stand up, only to get slapped in the face by Miko. I don't flinch, just slightly rub my cheek. "Nice," I say.

"I-I," she stutters.

"Drop the knife," I tell her, but her grip tightens . "Now," I say.

She turns the knife to me. "No. You are just like him." She attempts to take a step forward.

Before she can move, I grab her wrist, kick her inner knee enough to knock her down but not hurt as much, and snatch the knife away. "When I say now, I mean now," I tell her.

"God, what's happening to me?" She runs her hands through her hair.

I sit down next to her. "Miko, you snapped," I tell her.

"I just...I don't know what's happening to me. It's like all I can think about is death and killing and just anger," Miko says; she doesn't look at me.

I gently place my hand her shoulder. "Miko, look at me." She turns her head slowly, her eyes filled with tears on the verge of falling. "Now as I wanted to say, look around you, that's all this world is, death, destruction, anger, fear, all of it. It was only a matter of time before it consumed you. Now that it has, doesn't mean you lost complete control," I tell her.

"What?" she asks.

"You're losing control, you haven't lost all control. I'm not saying that it isn't gonna happen, but you control how it shapes you at least somewhat," I tell her. I know I'm bullshitting her right now, but it's not completely wrong. I understand what she is going through and how she feels. I felt like I was snapping after Kevin's death, and I still think I'm losing it, not because of that but just because it's bound to happen. It's hard to control who you become because, whether you like who you are or not, most of the time it's just who you are destined to be.

"I feel like you're telling me this just to make me feel better," she says. I can see tears start to form in her eyes, but not a single tear drips down at all.

"Maybe I am, but sometimes it's just what people need to hear," I tell her. That is true; sometimes it's better to hear what you want than the truth. It makes it slightly easier for the truth to come out.

She shakes her head. "I'm sorry I snapped," she says. She wipes her face like there are tears, but there aren't.

I grabbed both her shoulders. "You have nothing to apologize for to me, at least you didn't stab me. I'm the wrong person you should be apologizing to," I tell her.

"You're right. God, he probably hates me," she says.

"I highly doubt it, but go talk to him before you make things worse," I say, and she gets up to leave. When she is gone, I sprawl out on the floor. "God! If you're listening, take me!" I whisper-yell. This, I don't wanna do this anymore. I know I just basically lied to Miko, but I snapped a long time ago, before I even got with them. I just thought it went away until Kev's death and I realized who I still was, a broken, angry, and shattered person. I never knew someone could snap more than once, but it happened to me, and I feel like it's happening to Miko. I don't want that to happen to her. I wanna do whatever I can to help her, but it's happening, and I can't stop it, so all I can do is support and help. I grab the knife and look at it. It has dried blood on it, but some parts are still wet. It's a clean-cut knife; it must be the one she cooks with. I sit up and lean my back against the wall. I wonder how easy it would be to just turn the knife on myself right now. They probably wouldn't see since they are helping Alex. I could slit my throat, stab my chest, slit my wrist, so many options, but then I think about it. Losing a family to gain a sense of escape isn't worth it. I throw the knife away again.

"Hey…" Allison says and sits next to me.

"Yeah, hey," I say.

"I was thinking about having a conversation with Miko. This was…he may not be able to use his arm properly ever again. It was his right arm. So who else is gonna go out then?" she says.

"Let's not forget that you kil—"...I'm not even gonna say what she just did.

"That was different, sorta." She shrugs. "Anyway, I could use some back up," she asks.

"Maybe later. I'm gonna go check on Alex." I stand up, dust myself off, and walk away. I'm not in the mood to argue with anyone. I enter the medical office and lean against the doorway. Alex is lying down, his arm bandaged and hanging off his side; the kid is asleep. This may not be the best time to check up on him, but I want to make sure he is okay. He looks really pale and sweaty. I really hope he didn't catch an infection because we don't need to add being deadly sick on top of anything. It already sucks that he is gonna have to learn to defend himself with his left hand. Right when I'm about to leave, I hear him start coughing. I look over my shoulder, and it looks like there is some blood with whatever he is coughing up. "Hey, how are you feeling?" I ask and sit in the chair next to him.

He groans. "Like shit."

I touch his forehead and sure enough I was right, he is burning up. There must be an infection. "Did Allison give you any antibiotics?" I ask.

"No." He rolls over again and throws up. "She cleaned the cut, stitched the wound and bandaged it, but she couldn't reach them." He points to the top shelf.

"I'll get them." I pull the chair over and stand on top of it, trying to reach the bottle. Why the fuck do we put our medications so high up! I grab the bottle and step off the chair. "Here." I take out two and give them to him.

"Thank you." He takes them dry and lies back down.

"We should probably talk about what happened," I tell him.

"Do we really need to?" he asks.

"Yes," I say.

"Fine. I don't wanna break up with her Miranda," he says.

"I'm not saying you have to, just you guys have to stop putting your hands on each other. Not only that, you have to stop treating her like she's five. Alex, we are in the middle of an apocalypse; whether you like it or not she needs to be able to fend on her own and not have to worry about you saving her," I explain. He is always wanting to be a hero and trying to prove himself to everyone.

"I know, Miranda." He sighs out and sits up. "It;s just, I'm the only guy left in this group. Fuck, I have a girlfriend in this group and I love all of you. I just want to make sure you guys are always protected and safe. So maybe I do baby you guys sometimes, but I was such a 'bad person' before all of this, and this was like a new start for me. Sounds so messed up but if it wasn't for this, I would be dead. I had you to live for before. You made me wanna be a better person, and now I have you guys to live for and I am a better person. I know that I am not perfect, and I'm actually far from it, but I'm trying to make myself right, for Allison, for Miko, and especially for you, Miranda. You knew me, the old me, before all of this. You've seen all my struggles, yet you still stood by me. I got kicked out by that group and you talked the others into leaving. I just don't wanna lose anyone else," he says.

"I get it, Alex, I do. But you need to realize that we are gonna be okay and are gonna just have to take things step by step." I hug him, and I feel the wetness on my shirt. It didn't take much knowledge to realize he was crying. I've seen him cry a few times, before all of this, when I would meet up with him when he was drunk and emotional or when he was having his own problems. "It's okay, Alex. You're doing a great job." I rub his back. After a couple of minutes, I pull away. "I'm gonna go try and get some rest," I tell him.

"I will," he says. "By the way, remember I asked you if you always had my back?" he asks.

"Yeah…" I trail off.

"I was gonna do something to Jordan's body, but I never got the chance." He sighs. "I just didn't want him there, but now after this happening and the fact that I could still die from this, I realize I wouldn't want that for me."

"I'm glad your eyes are open, but seriously, get some rest," I tell him.

"Okay, see you later," he says.

I leave the room and go straight to my room and sit on my bed. "I wish I had a drink," I say. "Actually." I look under my bed. "Bingo!" I whisper and pull out a small bottle of vodka. "Forgot you were here," I say. Great, I am now the person who talks to inanimate objects. Before I take a sip, I hear through the door someone say, "You shouldn't be—" I can't make out the rest. "Of course today never ends." I sigh and follow the noise to Allison's room. I quietly see if the door is unlocked, and luckily, it is. I stand by the door, listening to Allison and Miko. It doesn't sound like they are arguing, but it sounds like there is a lot of tension in their voices.

"He saved your life, how could you do that?" Allison says.

"You're acting like I did it on purpose." I hear Miko suck her teeth.

"Still, you could have killed him, plus now what if he can't use his arm?" I hear Allison say.

"Well…well, at least I didn't kill two people!" Miko yells. Ouch, low blow.

"That's different!" Allison yells. Now is where the argument starts to pick up.

"No it's not! You killed because you snapped and reacted, just like I did. I know I made a mistake, but you don't have to keep rubbing it in my face. We didn't do that after you killed not one but two of our friends," Miko says.

"If I knew Miranda would go for it, I would kick you out this group right now," Allison says. Oh shit…

"Maybe I could do a disappearing trick like you did." I hear Miko laugh.

"I can't believe I ever believed in you!" Allison yells.

"Yeah, well, I can't believe we thought you would be a good leader…" I hear Miko's voice getting faint, still full of anger but lower.

"Well, I'm in charge, and I think your attitude has been totally unacceptable," Allison tells her.

"Yeah, and you're so much better," Miko says.

"At least I almost didn't kill my boyfriend!" Allison says.

"At least I still have a relationship!" Miko yells. Damn, that one hurt me. "I didn't break up with him because some blast from the past had a tantrum and I wouldn't take my partner's side. Instead, you told her not to do anything, and that's why everyone's life was put at risk when we played that stupid-ass game," Miko explains.

"Get out," Allison demands.

"Make me," Miko says, so, yep, my time to step in. I burst open the door in time to see Allison with a knife to Miko's throat.

"What the fuck is up with all the damn knives!" I yell. "Drop it, Allison. Don't make me say it again. I'm really not in the mood," I say.

She hands it to me, and I throw it outside the room. Allison takes a step back, and Miko pushes her, making her stumble back. "Are you kidding?" Allison tries to go for Miko, but I grab her and hold them both back.

This is getting on my nerves. I force both of them to sit down on the floor. "Okay, children! Stop," I tell them. "You guys are supposed to be family. I get family argues, but goddamn. Guys, both of you are getting way too out of hand." It's time for me to take complete leadership. "Miko, I don't know what the fuck happened to you, but you need to stay in your room for the next couple of days. You can come out to eat and people can go into your room twice a day maximum, but you need time alone," I tell her.

"Okay." She's looking down again like a puppy. "That is reasonable" she mumbles.

"Now, Allison. This. Has. To. Stop. You're co-leader for Christ's sake! Your decisions recently have either been too far off to work or you just haven't seen to be interested. It also just sounded like you were trying to abuse your power. So you are on temporary out-of-leadership duty until you realize how important it is," I tell her.

"Fine," she says shakily.

"I'm doing this for both of you. Now both apologize, because right now we should be even closer and be there for our friend who is in really bad shape right now," I tell them.

They look into each other's eyes. "I'm so sorry, Allison," Miko speaks first.

"I'm so sorry too, Miko," Allison says, and they hug.

"Good. Now your 'punishments' start now, so, Miko, please go to your room," I demand. She rushes out of the room. "And you, I can't even." I wave her off and walk out. What Miko said reminded me of the day Allison and I broke up, and it hurt. I just wish things could have different or at least we could talk about it, but it seems like we would just rather ignore it. I'll admit things went back to "normal," but it's harder than I thought trying to get over these feelings. It used to be easy for me to forget feelings, but not this one, though…. Vodka time.

When I wake up the next morning I have a pounding headache, but there is a knock at my door. I hear Allison say, "Can I come in?"

I mumble a quick, "Sure," and she comes in.

"Wow, where the hell did you find alcohol?" she asks.

"I found it on my last hunting trip. Figured we didn't need everyone to have the bottle again, so I drank it," I say, and pull out two aspirin and swallow them.

"Well, breakfast is done, and I was hoping to make a suggestion about our next move," Allison says.

"No," I shut her down and stand up. "Whatever it is can wait until you are back in power, so let's go eat," I say. While walking down the hall, I knock on Miko's door. "Hey! Breakfast!" I shout.

"I'm not hungry!" I hear her yell back. I don't want to argue.

We are so empty here now. I wish we had more people or our people back. I grab a bowl of oatmeal and some berries and take it to my room. I don't think anyone is in the mood for each other. Maybe I was too harsh on the girls considering what we have been getting put through but after they had a fight with each other they need to fix themselves. We all spend most of the days in our rooms because, one, it was raining really bad and, two, because no one wanted to speak. I'm currently tapping my pencil of my desk trying to write something. Since I'm not used to writing like that, I figured I'll write a diary and maybe my skills will fall back. I titled my diary "It's all over." Basic but it's how I have been feeling. It's another hour into writing and I hear a bang from the air vents. "God what now." I groan loudly and get up to check out where the noise has come from.

When I'm about to go back into my room, I hear, "Let go of me!" It sounds like it's Alex, and it sounds like it's coming from Miko's room. I go knock on the door and I hear a loud smack and I pull out my dagger. "I told you let go!" That's definitely Alex.

I bust open the door and I see Miko hugging her knees, tears jerking in her eyes but none are falling, and a big handprint on the side of her face. Fuck, I never saw Alex hit a girl before. He is usually good at not putting his hands on us. I know he has gotten into physical altercations with females. Hell, me and him got into me but never… Out of instinct I rush to the floor and place my hands on Miko's knees. "Look at me," I ask, and she shakes her head, buries her head into her knees.

"Miko, I'm so sorry, babe." Alex tries to step to her, and I clench my fist and stand up slowly. "Miranda." He hesitates.

I turn around and punch him in the face. He stumbles due to shock, and he grabs his jaw. I grab him by his shirt and slam him up against her wall. "You should know better than anyone that I'm a woman of my word. Now get the fuck out her room now, you fucking piece of shit." I throw him out the room. I shut the door and return to Miko. "He's gone," I tell her.

All of a sudden, she looks up. "I'm fine." She stands up and dusts herself off. "Don't worry about me." She smiles. *Not like her old ones.*

"I know you're lying to me," I tell her.

"How?" she asks.

"Honestly, I pay attention; you have different gestures, different smiles, even different glints in your eyes. You had a smile in school, but never like your smile on the phone. You had a smile when this whole thing happened, you have a smile when you are talking to each of us differently. The smile and shift in your body flashed back to your school smile, and I didn't like that one. I like the smile you have when we are talking or the one when the group is hanging out," I explain, and she looks taken aback.

"I don't know what you're talking about," she says.

"At least tell me what happened," I ask.

"He came in trying to lecture me about my behavior, and one thing led to another, and I pushed him. He ended up banging his back on my bedpost. He put his hand in my face, I grabbed his hand and tried to push him out, and he slapped me," she explains.

"What happened to you guys?" They were so mushy.

"I guess after the spark left, we dimmed out and true colors came out. Now, Miranda, I'm fine. Please leave me alone," she begs, and I nod.

"I'm taking your punishment off now. Something tells me you being alone is making you worse. I'll see you tomorrow morning," I tell her and walk out. I go straight to Alex's room and bang on his door. "Get the hell outside, now." I bang one more time and go out in the rain.

He comes out shortly after. "I'm sor—" I don't let him finish his sentence and I punch him again and tackle him.

In between punches I was speaking, "You"—hit one—"are"—hit two— "supposed"—hit three—"protect"—hit four. Before I can hit him again, I see him trying to grab his gun and I grab it and place it to his head. "Fuck you," I say.

"I know I fucked up, but please, let me fix this," he begs.

"I told you if you ever touched—" I'm cut off by voices in the forest.

"Help, please help us!" I hear a male voice yell. Alex grabs the gun and pushes me off. He runs into the building. I stand up and see three people standing outside the gate, this man around forty, one teenage boy, and a little boy, no older than eight most likely.

I go to the gate. "What do you want?" I ask.

"Please, can I talk to the person who is in charge of your group?" the man says. I guess he assumes that kids can't be in charge.

"You're talking to her." I fold my arms.

He looks stunned. "Uh, well, aren't you a bit young to be in charge?" Is this guy serious? He wants help and is talking shit.

"If you don't want help then get the hell out of here." I shrug and am about to walk away.

"Wait, please!" the little boy asks, and I stop. My heart jerks at the sound of the boy's voice.

"What do you need?" I ask without turning around. I feel something drip from my hand. I realize my knuckles are bleeding; usually water stings it, but I don't feel anything.

The man speaks. "I don't care about me, but please, take my kids," he begs. "We haven't eaten in days, my kids are exhausted. Please, I'll do anything."

I turn and face him. "How do I know you're telling the truth? For all I know you're a part of a group and will come back here and hurt my people" I say and the rain starts getting heavier.

"Please, let us in," the older boy says.

I pull out my gun and point it at the man. "Fine, all of you come in." I open the gate. "All of you on your knees," I order, and the three of them do as I say. I don't like doing this to people, but nowadays, my family comes first, and I'll do anything to protect them. "This is gonna be quick and easy. Put your hands behind your head, and if any of you try anything I won't hesitate," I say.

"I can't believe it. You're so young," the man tells me.

"Shut up," I say and go to the little boy first, not expecting to find anything. "Hey, what's your name?" I ask him

"I'm Jake! And I'm seven!" he says.

"He is pure, hard to see that now," I tell the father. "Little one, get up."

He stands up and I pat him down; sure enough I don't find anything but a toy race car. "Next is you. What's your name and age?" I ask the older boy.

"I'm Daniel, and I'm probably twenty-two now." Damn, he is way older than us. Alex is the oldest, and he is twenty, then me, I'm nineteen, but a few months older than Allison, then Miko, she's eighteen. I search him and find a switchblade, I put the switchblade in my back pocket and a map.

"What's the map for?" I ask.

"It was to help us walk through the forest; it doesn't really work," Daniel speaks.

I nod and move to the dad. "Age, name."

"Robert and I'm forty-six." I search him and find a gun but with no bullets, so I throw it to the side. I also find a picture of who I'm gonna assume is the mom and I put it back.

"Miranda, what the fuck is going on!" Allison runs out.

"Don't worry about it," I tell her. She looks at the little boy, and she frowns.

"They can all stay," Allison tells me.

"Uh, you don't have a say at the moment, remember?" I tell her.

The realization hit her. "Oh yeah." She sighs.

"You guys can stay I guess, but I'd like to speak to each of you one-on-one first," I tell them.

"Of course, let me just talk to my sons first," Robert says and drags the boys away. I see out of the corner of my eye what looks like him reprimanding the boys.

"Fuck that, I need to speak to the little one first!" I shout, and his head jerks up and glares at me before pushing Jake up slightly to speak. The little boy runs over.

"Come with me," I tell him and bring him into the office.

"Am I in trouble?" Jake asked.

"No, I just have to ask you some questions," I tell him. "First, how long have you been on the road?" I ask.

"A very long time," he answers. "Do you wanna play toy cars with me?" Cute kid.

"Not right now. Where is your mom?" I ask.

He looks nervous about this question. "Oh, uh, Mommy, uh, Mommy is gone," he stutters out.

I bend down to his level. "Does your father take care of you like he is supposed to?" I ask.

"Of course! I mean sometimes before, no, never mind, Daddy is nice," he says. Sometimes before?

"Now I got a job for you. I need you to run and get your brother and bring him right here. You think you can do that?" He nodded excitedly. "Good" I gave him a high five.

I sit on the desk and run my hand through my hair. I miss my little brother. But that man seems well enough to stay. There are just some things I'm not too sure about, but that's why I'm hoping Daniel can clear some of this up. Jake bursts open the door. "I got him!" he yells. I give him a thumbs up and he runs off.

"Ignore my brother. I try to save his innocence. You're really pretty." Daniel smiles at me.

"Awesome. Now let's get back to the question," I tell him. I don't need any more feelings involved, especially with a newcomer.

"Sharpshooter, respect," he says.

"When was the last time you guys ate?" I ask.

"Honestly?" He looks behind him to make sure the door is closed. "We ate yesterday, but Robert—I mean Dad thought you guys wouldn't let us in," he says.

"You call your dad by his first name?" I ask; now that's weird.

"Sorry, it blurted out since you don't know us," he tried to explain.

"What's the map for?"

"Marking where we think is dangerous. Look whatever happens, please just protect my br—" He gets cut off by the door bursting open and Robert coming in with a huge smile on his face. Daniel immediately stands straight.

"I didn't mean to interrupt but I wanted to let Daniel know his brother is misbehaving and he should talk to him." Robert laughs and puts his hand on Daniel's shoulder.

"Of course. Dad." Daniel runs off.

"They are good kids," Robert tells me.

"Yeah, they look like it. You seem like you teach them well," I tell him.

"I try, but boy, if I thought raising them in normal life was hard, this is way harder," he tells me.

"Yeah, well, all of us need to grow up sooner or later," I say. "You and your boys can stay, of course. But your boys, including Jake, need to be able to help around. The room right next to mine is free; go in that one with your boys," I explain.

He shakes my hand. "Thank you so much."

"Anytime. You can go tell the boys the good news," I tell him, and he leaves, and Allison walks in.

"Miranda?" She comes in.

"What's up?" I ask.

"I want to apologize, for everything that has been happening. Especially with us, because I never expected for us to get this bad or awkward and I'm so sorry for my behavior," she says.

Miko walks in. "I broke up with Alex," she says.

"Woah, wait, what?" Allison says.

"I don't think we are gonna work," she says.

"Are you okay?" I ask.

"Yeah, fine. Just figured I would let you know. I'll leave you two now." She leaves. I hope things won't get any weirder now.

"Now back to what I was saying," Allison says, snapping me back into our conversation.

"What exactly are you saying?" I ask.

She wraps her arms around my neck. "I want to get back together with you, Miranda. I still like you so much, and I didn't want to break up. Plus, I hate how things have been going with us. So, what do you say?" She looks uncertain and scared.

"I-I'm not sure, Allison. I do like you still, but the group is the most important right now and I don't want the risk of another break-up to ruin it." I sigh.

"Please," she begs.

"No." I take her arms off of me. "Now please get out and have Miko start cooking," I say.

She leaves looking hurt.

"Hey, can we play toy cars now?" Jake comes in, and I laugh.

"Of course, kiddo." I sit with him on the floor.

Are we a home?

It's only been two days and Alex only comes out to hunt and eat, the boys are training with me, and the dad doesn't come out of his room, ever. It is a little weird, but he is a nice guy; he is always making sure the kids help out, and sometimes I see the kids bringing him food. It's almost time to go hunting, and today, Daniel is going to try and come with Miko and me; Alex is sick. "Guys, are you ready to head out?" I ask.

"Let's go, boss," Daniel says

"Yeah, I'll go scout ahead and make sure the space outside the gate is clear for us to run," Miko says and runs out.

"Daniel!" Robert comes outside, the first time in these two days. "You better be on your BEST behavior; you don't want to cause any trouble." Robert nods.

"Of course," Daniel says with a sure nod.

"Be careful. I'm gonna take Jake to pick some vegetables real quick, then go on watch," Allison tells me.

"Daniel, let's go," I tell him, and we go off and meet with Miko. "Come on, children," I tell them.

"Uhhh, I'm twenty-two," Daniel points out.

"But I'm in charge," I tell him.

"Touché," he says.

"So, what are we looking for today?" Miko asks.

"Honestly, whatever we can find," I tell her.

"No fishing?" she asks.

"Nah, not today," I say.

A couple of minutes of not finding anything, we spot a raccoon. "Look!" Daniel points.

"Miko, this one is all you. I don't want rabies." I laugh.

"Great, so much love." She rolls her eyes and takes her bow and arrow out. She takes a deep breath. "Fuck, I don't want to miss," she says.

I stand and help. "It's fine. Just keep a clear head," I tell her. I notice her hands are shaking slightly, but she doesn't want me to see. "Here." I place my hands on hers. "I'm just helping, don't worry." I line her hands up and step back. "Now shoot." She lets go of the arrow and hits the raccoon dead on. "See? Nothing to worry about."

"Hey, nice hit." Daniel high-fives Miko.

"I wasn't nervous, just cautious," she says.

"But your hands were shaking," I say.

"No they weren't." Why is she denying it? It's okay to be a little nervous from time to time.

"Uh, okay? Daniel, go get it." I motion for him to get the dead raccoon, and he runs to get it.

"I appreciate your help with the bow, Miranda, but I could have gotten it," she says.

"Sure you could, but at least we did it," I say. Something with her is off, dry. It's like she shut down, like a robot that is malfunctioning.

Daniel comes running back with the raccoon in his hand. "Boom!" He waves it around.

"Okay, weirdo, let's get back," I tell him, and we all chuckle. When we get back, their dad isn't out again. Damn, I really want Miko to meet him; she's the only one who hasn't met him yet.

"How was everything while we were gone?" I ask Allison up on watch 'cause I notice a couple dead zombies around the gates.

"Pretty chill. We had a few zombies walking around. Alex took care of them actually. Then Alex locked himself back into his room. I think he's getting sick still." She sighs.

"Let me talk to you for a sec," I tell her and motion to the side. "Daniel, give the raccoon to Allison, and Miko, go practice your bow and arrow," I order them both. Allison jumps down and we walk to the side. "You have the first night lookout shift with Miko, right?" I ask.

"Yeah, why?" she asks.

"Let me take the next shift with her," I tell her. I need to figure out what the hell is going on with Miko.

"Sure, boss." She salutes.

"Don't call me…" I tell her.

"Okay...boss." Before I can say anything she runs off.

I go to check on Alex. My knuckles are still scratched up. I have no idea what I'm going to do with this kid. At the end of the day, he is family, is always there for us, good with a gun, and overall is good with surviving this shit, but his actions recently are gonna get him or one of us killed. He is being reckless with his hands and mouth, the girls too. That's why they got punishments, but him, it's harder since he is a guy. I can't exactly tell him to go in timeout and not feel awkward about it. Part of me wants to kick him out because of thinking long term, but the other part is remembering the two years on the road we all faced and all the shit the group has been through and how a small string of screw ups are gonna just throw it all away. "Alex," I say.

"Miranda," he says.

"I am only going to say this once, this is your LAST chance. You come out your mouth or dare to raise your hand to a girl again, I'll put a bullet in your head. I don't want anything bad to happen to you, hell, you're lucky I don't kick you out now. But you're banned from hunting until further notice," I tell him.

"What!" He sits up. "You can't be serious."

"I am. Now feel better." I walk out and hear him throwing up again.

"Miranda, the shift is about to start," Jake runs in to tell me.

"Thank you. Hey, do you know how to work a gun?" I ask.

"Uhhhh no." He looks wide-eyed and shakes his head.

"I didn't think so. Maybe you're too young for that. You need to train for something though," I tell him, and he shrugs, and I wave him off. I go outside. "Miko, lookout time!" I yell.

"I thought it was me and Allison?" she asks.

"Well, now it's me and you." I grab a bowl of food. "Let's go," I tell her.

When we get to the top, we eat in silence for a long time; no one speaks until we are both done eating. "Why did you have Allison switch?" she asks.

"Because I want to know what is going on with you," I tell her, and she looks out into the distance.

"I'm fine, Miranda," she says.

"Look me in the face and tell me you're fine," I tell her. *I know she can't do that.*

She looks at me. "I'm fine," but she cracks and looks down before finishing her sentence.

"You're a bad liar," I say.

"DROP. IT!" she yells.

I hold my hands up in defense. "You loud!" I hear Jake.

"Go away, Jake!" I yelled down to him. "I'm just worried about you." I turn back to her.

"I know. It's just my mind playing tricks on me. I keep thinking I'm seeing this guy around, but I'm not sure. And all this uncertainty is bringing up past memories that I don't like talking about," she says.

"You want a hug?" I ask, and she nods weakly and hugs me. "I'm here for you, we are all here for you, Miko. Even Alex," I tell her.

"I know." She sighs and pulls away.

"So, are you liking the new boys?" I ask.

"Yeah, honestly Daniel seems pretty cool, laid back, quiet, and mysterious. It's cool yet alarming, like, what skeletons are in his closet? But with that being said, that could just be his personality. Jake, he is just adorable. What about you?" she asks.

"Daniel seems like once he gets comfortable, he will be a fun guy to hang out with. I agree with the whole quiet and mysterious thing. Jake, well. He reminds me of my little brother, and it hurts, but at the same time it brings a little joy that they brought my brother back in another form," I tell her.

"Yeah, having a little kid around is so weird but refreshing because he is so innocent," she says.

"I mean we did almost have a baby on our hands." I laugh, and she punches my shoulder.

"Not funny." She rolls her eyes.

"It is hilarious," I tell her. "Was he at least good?"

"Oh my god, I am so done with this conversation." She laughs.

We stop the conversation there for right now and just sit looking out in the distance. There are a few zombies, dragging their feet slowly towards the east, but nothing to be worried about, so we just stare out. "The sun will be setting soon," I say.

"Yeah, this is my favorite shift," she tells me.

"I know. You always call it," I say.

"How are you and Allison?" she asks.

"I mean, we are still friends and decided to give each other some space and just be friendly." I shrug.

"You sound so blah with it," she says.

"I don't think of it like that. I think of it how it is, and I try not to think about it and just let us play out like it is supposed to be." The conversation dies out again, and the sun starts setting. I look down at the group and see Robert come out again. "Miko, there's someone I want you to meet!" We climb down.

MIKO'S POV

Miranda and I go down the ladder before our shift is over for some reason. She is always trying to be there for everyone, and sometimes I feel like she spreads herself too thin to hide her own demons. But I still love her, but I won't tell her; it's more fun to bother her. Who the hell could she want me to meet? I thought it was just the two boys. "Miranda, our shift...isn't—" I stop short when I am eye to eye with the man she wants to meet. My thoughts weren't playing tricks on me, he is here....

MIRANDA'S POV

"Miranda, our shift...isn't—" Miko cuts herself off and just stares at Robert.

"Miko, this is Robert, the boys' father. Robert, this is Miko. She is a really good strategist and amazing with a bow," I introduce them.

"It's a pleasure," Robert says with a huge smile and holds out his hand.

Miko is just frozen in place, you would swear she saw a ghost. "Miko." I tap her shoulder.

"Nice to meet you, I uh, we need to finish the lookout shift," Miko says, and she grabs my hand and races up the ladder. When we reach the top of the spot, Miko starts hyperventilating "I-I just l-l-let me be," she stutters out through every breath.

"Miko, you don't look okay." I sit in front of her,

"J-Just give me a se-second," she says, and I place my hands on her knees.

"Close your eyes, put your head down, and breathe with me," I tell her, and she follows what I said. After five minutes she calms down. "Now tell me what's going on," I ask.

"Well, I don't want to go into the long story right now. Just please never ever leave me alone with that guy." She breathes out.

"I should know why I have to protect you," I tell her.

"Miranda, please…not now." She sighs and leans back.

It's clear I'm now going to find out what the problem is right now. She probably recognizes him from the past, and by the looks of it, he wasn't very good to her. An old teacher? An old babysitter? A bad guy overall? I hand her my dagger. "Keep this next to you. I know you had one, but that one is in my room, so use mine." She takes it reluctantly.

"I prefer mine." She swings it in the air. "Yours is too big for my hand, but it should work for now, until I get mine back, of course," she tells me.

The sun is completely set. "It's time to switch shifts. Daniel and Allison have it now," I tell her. I'm starting to think this "perfect little family" Robert has, has more skeletons in their closet than I can count.

"I think I can get Daniel to tell me anything. I'm almost positive he has a crush on me," I tell her.

"Perfect, get intel and we can figure everything out from there," she says.

"Until then, go to bed and we will continue all of this tomorrow." We hop off the lookout thing and send the other two back up. When we are walking back to our rooms, Alex is leaving his, and him and Miko freeze. "Look, we aren't doing this," I say.

"Miko, I'm sorry for ever putting my hands on you. If you want to stay away from me or we just keep a distance, I totally understand, but I still care about you, and I want you to know I got your back no matter what, because you are still my family," he explains to her.

A faint smile forms on her lips. "Thank you. Alex and I am sorry for everything I did, the knife, grabbing you. I should never have put my hands on you, and hell, I never should have sliced you, and I'm so glad it's getting better. I hope we can be the friends we were before," she tells him. Yeah, his arm is sore for him to keep moving it up and down, so he is practicing by fighting hand-to-hand, but his gun skills are getting back to normal.

"Now that this is settled, Miko has a very bad feeling about the dad of the two boys. She won't tell me why she doesn't like him, but they have a bad history, so be careful and have her back," I explain to him.

"You need anything, I am right across the hall. Say anything and I'll break down a door if I have to. Now if you excuse me, I haven't eaten all day." He walks past us.

"Keep the dagger under the pillow and the gun beside you, please." I hug her. "Stay safe," I tell her.

She opens her door. "Always." And I walk to my room.

I plop on my bed and hear a giggle. "What the fuck?" I say, sitting up.

"That's a swear!" Jake comes out from under my bed. "I usually sleep with my brother but he has that lookout thingy now, so I don't know where to go." He sits with me.

"You can stay with me," I tell him.

"Really!?" He bounces up and down. "Don't tell anyone but you're my most favorite," he whispers.

"Don't worry, secret safe." I put my finger to my lips. "Come lie down, let's sleep," I tell him, and we lie down together and fall asleep. Halfway through the night I hear Jake tossing and turning mumbling something. I try my best to make out what he is saying.

"No, I'm sorry. I am good! Go away! No hurt me! No hurt Daniel, Daddy!" he starts whispering/yelling. I gently shake him up, and he sits up crying. "Is it just a bad dream?" Jake asks.

"Yeah, it's okay. Why would Daddy hurt you?" I ask.

"I am not allowed to say. If I say, Daniel gets hurt," he says.

What the hell? Why would Daniel get hurt? I don't know who you are, Robert. But I will find out. I stayed up the rest of the night making sure Jake was okay. When the sun is fully risen, I gently shake him. "Hey, little man. It's bright and early to start a new day," I say, and he wakes up slowly.

"But I'm still tired," he whines.

"Well, maybe if you get up now you can help Miko cook breakfast," I tell him, and he jumps up in excitement.

I hear a knock on the door, and before I could say anything, Robert walks in. "Good morning, Miranda. Is Jake here?" he asks.

I put on a fake smile. "Yeah, he wasn't feeling good so I let him stay with me," I tell him.

"I'm here." Jake runs to Robert.

"Good boy." Robert ruffles Jake's hair. "I was worried you went too far," he says.

"We really should be heading out. I told Jake he could help Miko cook breakfast," I tell Robert.

"Be careful this little sucker doesn't burn the school down." Robert laughs; his laugh sounds like a hyena dying. "I think I'll go out too. It's a beautiful day, and I haven't been out much," he says with a smug smile.

"Uh, sure," I say, and we all leave my room and head outside. Daniel is talking to Allison, and Miko just started the fire, while Alex is on watch. Before anything can clash, I run to Miko. "Hey, trust me." I grab her hand and drag her to the garden.

"Miranda, what the fuck?" She yanks her hand away.

Ooh, cursing. "I just want you to know that Robert is coming out and I want to make sure you're comfortable with it, because if you're not, I will get him to leave," I explain to her.

She shifts uncomfortably. "No, it's fine." She half-smiles. "Just uh, stick by me at all times." She grabs my arm.

"Got it," I tell her, and we head back to the group. Allison is now cooking. I put my hand on her shoulder. "Morning. After breakfast I'll announce what everyone is doing," I tell her.

"Sounds good." She continues cooking. Now let's get some information.

I drag Miko with me to Daniel and Jake play fighting "Miko, I promise I'll be right here, but right now can you go just over by Allison. I'll come to get you when I'm done talking to Daniel," I say. At first she is hesitant and clings to my arm harder. "Now, before you draw blood." I laugh.

She laughs and lets go. "Okay, don't forget about me." She runs off and starts talking to Allison and helping her cook.

"Jake, I got a VERY big job for you," I tell him.

"Oh, what! I wanna help!" He bounces up and down.

"I need you to go all around the school front and find flowers," I tell him.

"I can do that!" He runs off.

"Hey, Daniel." I smile at him.

"Hey, Miranda." He gives this big cheeky smile, like he just got candy or a reward from the store.

"I was wondering if you want to get to know each other a little?" I place my hand on his shoulder. "We are in the same group, after all," I ask. I feel bad for basically leading him on, but I want to know what's wrong with Robert, and I want to make sure Jake and Daniel are safe, and if fake flirting the way to go, then I'm sorry, Daniel; you will thank me later.

"I uh, I, yeah, o-of course!" he stutters out; his face is as red as a tomato and his smile only gets bigger. I guess he never really liked a girl, or a girl never liked him before.

"Great, meet me in my room tonight." I kiss his cheek.

"Breakfast's ready!" Allison and Miko yell.

Daniel is about to sit with us but, "Daniel!" Robert yells. Daniel jumps. "You really were about to leave your old pop all alone?" he asks. I don't understand...like at all. He seems like a nice guy.

"Of course not, Pop." He sighs and sits with Robert. Alex comes down from watch and I signal for him to sit with Daniel to watch him, and he nods. Throughout breakfast, Daniel keeps side-eyeing me and sighing. I could have sworn I saw Robert touch Daniel's knee, but I think it's just what Miko said that's getting to me again.

"Miranda, are you okay? You have been distracted all day," Allison asks.

"Yeah, I'm fine, don't worry." I wave my hand slightly. "Just having an off day." I smile.

"So, I was thinking, how about Miko, me, and Jake go fishing?" I tell the table.

"Oooh fishy!" Jake claps.

"Absolutely." Miko smiles in relief.

"Allison, take Daniel and Alex to go check on the green house. Oh and explain to Robert how to do a lookout shift," I tell her. I finish eating and go to Daniel's table. "Hey, guys. Allison is gonna need you two at the green house today, and Robert, you're gonna be a lookout today while everyone is gone," I explain.

"I want to go hun—" Alex starts.

"Don't," I tell him.

"Sounds perfect, Miranda." Daniel smiles, and I smile back.

"Yep," Robert chimes in.

"Okay so—" I try to start but Allison runs up. Yo this fucking girl! I'm gonna duct tape her mouth shut one day.

"Hey, everyone! You boys ready to go?" she asks. They both nod and get up. "Let's go," she gestures, and they leave.

"So, Miranda," Robert says, "please have a seat," he gestures, and I sit down slowly.

"Yes?" I ask.

"You think I'm a good guy?" he asks, and I nod slowly. "I see you have taken an interest in my son. Well, with kissing his cheek and everything." When I'm about to say something, "Stop, I see everything." He puts his hand up. "It looks like you have an interest in a few people, or at least some people have an interest in you," he says. Is this man really trying to say what I think he is?

"I don't know what you are talking about with 'other people,' and even if I did, that is none of your concern," I tell him.

"Of course. I heard you and that girl Allison used to date. Sweet girl. I also heard you went on a few dates with that boy Alex. I totally understand. I just want you to understand Daniel is a fragile little boy on the inside, and if it wasn't for me, he wouldn't be the man he was today. *He needed a guy to make him a man,*" he says. Wait a sec…

"Did you just say a guy? Don't you mean his dad?" I ask. I can see his eyes go wide.

"That's what I mean, you know, old age." He laughs it off. I'm not laughing, Robert.

"And secondly, yes, Allison and me dated, Alex had a thing for me, so I went on some dates to see if there was a spark, and for your information, there wasn't, but it isn't any of your business." I clench my fist. "Lastly, whatever the fuck I do is up to me, so don't you dare tell me what to do, because in case you forgot, you are in MY group, not yours. You don't like the way things are run, then you can gladly get the fuck out. I don't care," I tell him. He looks taken aback for a moment, then quickly regains his composure.

"I'm so sorry for overstepping my boundary. Truce?" He holds his hand out and I shake it. "I'll go ask Allison about that lookout thing." He gets up and starts to move to the table.

"Miranda! Can we go, please?" Miko comes up and hides slightly behind me. Robert, seeing her, stops dead in his tracks.

"Miko, is it? You're a very pretty young lady." Robert smiles, and Miko digs her nails into my arm.

"Robert, just go to Allison," I tell him. Once he is gone, I tap Miko's hand. "Uh you're drawing blood," I tell her, and she lets go quickly.

"Uh, shit," she whispers, hoping I wouldn't hear it. "I'm so sorry." She pulls out Band-Aids, but I stop her.

"Don't worry, it's just some little scratches," I tell her. "Come on, we really should be going." I tell her and grab her hand. "Jake, buddy, come on!" I grab his hand too. "Come on, kids." I laugh, and Miko just rolls her eyes. We walk to the river…well, Miko and I walk, Jake keeps running ahead. "Jake, stop! You gotta be careful!" I yell out to him, and he stops.

"Look at you." Miko shoves me slightly, "Ms. Mom." She laughs.

"Yeah, who knew I could do it." I laugh. Before this started ,I always said I didn't want kids, because my little brother was a pain in the ass to take care of. Yeah, my parents and sister wasaround, but my mom couldn't do much, and my dad was a douche, so it was kind of like just me and him. I didn't treat my brother the way I should, and now it's too late. I won't mess up again.

"I did," Miko says.

"What?" I snapped back to reality.

"Nothing." She pats my back, and we finally catch up to Jake. "Now, I'll race you and Jake to the river." She laughs and takes off running.

"Come on, Jake." I grab his hand and we start running. We are neck and neck to Miko, but Jake is dragging me down. "Come here." I pick him up and he holds on, and I run as fast as I can, just passing Miko to the river. "Ayyyyy. We. won" I pant and put Jake down.

"Damn it." She sits. "We shouldn't have done that" she says through heavy breathes.

"Probably not." I laugh. "Come on, lazy ass, get up. We didn't run over here to sit down." I hold a hand out and help pull her up.

"I wanna catch the fish!" Jake says.

"Okay, buddy." I grab three spears. "This is very sharp, so you gotta be careful." I hand him the spear. "Look, follow my lead." I demonstrate how to plunge the spear in the water, and he does it the same way. "Good job." I high-five Jake.

"Can I get mine?" Miko holds her hand out.

"Isn't it too big for you?" I smirk, and she pushes me into the water. "Miko, what the fuck!" I yell; now I'm soaked.

"Don't underestimate short people." She snatches the spear and blows a kiss.

"I don't like you," I tell her.

"Aww, thanks." She goes to a spot.

"I wanna get wet," Jake says.

"No," I tell him.

"But…but," he whines.

"I said no, Jake." I turn to try and fish.

"You're mean!" Jake throws the spear down and stomps away.

"Jake, you get back here right now!" I yell after him, but he keeps walking. "Miko, stay here," I tell her, and she nods. I run after Jake; now I remember why I didn't want kids. "Jake, stop!" I shout.

"NO!" he screams and turns to me. "You mean!" He tears up.

"I just didn't want you to get all wet; it's getting too cold for that," I tell him. I see one of the zombies coming after Jake. "Jake, move," I tell him, but he doesn't. "I'm serious, come here," I say.

"No." He shakes his head. I pull out my gun and shoot the zombie behind him.

"Fuck, that was loud." I look all over. I go and grab Jake's hand. "We gotta move, now." I drag him with me and run to the river.

"Miranda, are you okay? I heard a gunshot?" Miko asks, holding the bucket.

"Yeah, on the safe side we better get back," I tell her.

"Miranda, we don't have enough for everyone today. Even with what Allison is to bring back, no way I can make three fish and vegetables enough for eight people. Especially because we are saving the can stuff until tomorrow when we can go looking for more," she says.

"We will figure it out when we get back," I say. That's never happened before. We always had enough or tried to make it work with the six of us, whether it was cut in half or eat more vegetables. At times it was hard, but no one went to bed hungry. Well, when we didn't feel like eating we did. Sometimes me, Miko, or Allison wouldn't want to eat, but that's different. This time everyone does and not everyone can.

…Times are changing…

We reach the school. Allison and the boys are returning from the greenhouse. "We got some ginger, carrots, and a couple other things," Allison says.

I sigh, taking a deep breath. "I have an announcement!" I climb on top of the table. "Today's fishing didn't go as planned, and well, there isn't enough for everyone to eat, and I decided that three people won't be eating tonight. It will be me, Robert, and whichever of the boys is willing." I gesture to Alex and Daniel.

"I'll do it!" they both say at the same time.

"Well, I wasn't expecting that, um…" I look around for help.

"I'll do it because it will prove I am willing to do what it takes for the group to stay and to show I care about you," Daniel says.

"I wanna be able to go hunting if I don't eat," Alex says.

"You wouldn't be doing this to get something in return, you would be doing this out of the best for the group," I tell Alex.

"So, the best of the group is the old man not eating?" Robert butts in.

"Yes, the kids work, you don't," I say.

"But that's not fair! You know I'm one of the best hunters here!" Alex starts getting louder.

"I don't know who you think you're talking to like that," Allison snaps back and steps up on the table with me. "Miranda said it has to be one of you, and it's gonna be you," Allison tells Alex. He huffs and storms to the rooms.

"Thanks." I hug her. "Now with that out of the way, Miko starts cooking for the rest." Allison and I jump down. "Allison, come here." I pull her to the side.

"Look, I know I overstepped my boundaries about the whole who is in charge and I'm sorry," she apologizes. "To be honest, I think you should stay in charge anyway," she says

"I uh, wow, you're serious?" I ask.

"Yeah, you have done amazing on your own, and I'm proud of you." She smiles and takes my hand.

"But I still need help," I tell her.

"News flash: we are in the same group. Of course I'll help. Think of me as your right hand, but you are now a full leader," she says. I decide to take a minute and go to my room for a moment of quiet and no interruptions. I sit on my bed and close my eyes, flashing to everything that's been happening, and the moments that have been changing us.

Allison: Victoria tries to beg Allison to stop, but she won't; instead, she puts the knife to her throat and starts cutting slowly as if she wanted to see all the blood drain from Victoria's face and body. We see Victoria's eyes roll in the back of her head, and she starts coughing up blood.

Miko: Miko turns around and stabs Alex in his arm and drags the knife down. "Ahhh fuck!" He pushes her away again and drops to his knees.

Me: In between punches I was speaking "You"—hit one—"are"—hit two— "supposed"—hit three—"protect"—hit four. Before I can hit him again, I see him trying to grab his gun, and I grab it and place it to his head. "Fuck you," I say.

"Miranda!" Jake knocks and opens my door.

"Hey, little man. Did you eat well?" I ask, and he nods slightly.

"Daddy really mad you didn't let him eat" Jake whimpers slightly and holds his stomach "he made me give him almost all my food, I still really hungry" he hugs me.

"Jake!" Daniel runs in "are you okay?" he panics "is he okay?" he asks me.

"Yeah, just hungry" I tell him.

Daniel looks at Jake and sighs. "Hey, bud, I have some food left, go finish mine." He nudges Jake's shoulder.

"Really? What about you?" Jake asks Daniel.

"Don't worry about it, little man, go eat." He motions to the table, and Jake runs off. Daniel stares at him running.

"You're a great big brother." I put a hand on his shoulder.

"Thank you," he says, but his eyes were still locked on Jake.

"Hey, what's wrong?" I ask.

"Jake has been getting in trouble so I'm just worried he will make uh, Dad snap," he says.

"Hey, it's later. Meet me in my room again when everyone else is in for the night," I tell him.

Time to figure out what's really going on

I'm sitting on my bed; my hands are shaking really bad but I'm sitting on them so he won't see them when he walks in. I'm not sure if I'm ready to hear what this guy did. Hell, I'm not even sure if Daniel is going to tell me. The timing is ticking down. I hear a soft knock on the door "Hey, Miranda, it's me!" Daniel whisper/yells.

"Come in!" I yell.

"Hey." He walks in and stands by the bed awkwardly.

"You know you can sit, right? I don't bite." I laugh.

"Oh yeah, right." He sits, leaving a gap between us.

"So, are you up for a little game?" I ask with a half smirk on my face.

"What game?" he asks.

I pull a pack of cards out from under my pillow. "War, but with a twist," I say.

"I'm not sure if I'll like this twist," he says, but I can tell he is trying to hide a smile.

"It's easy, whoever losses each round has to tell one thing or do a dare," I explain.

"Sounds fun." He claps his hands together.

"Oh! And since it's my rules, I can ask you two things or make you do a dare and a truth if I want." I grin evilly.

"That is so not fair." He rolls his eyes.

I start shuffling the deck pretending not to hear him. I'm actually really excited for this. Daniel is cute; he definitely looks like the friend-zoned boy in school, but at the same time he is amazing with combat and weapons. Plus, it looks like he has a nice body, just covered up all the time. I deal out the cards. "Ready to lose, nerd?" I try and taunt, but he just chuckles.

"Nerd, eh? Okay, dork." We both start laughing this time. We flip over the cards. I have a six of hearts, but he had a king of spades. "Truth. Biggest regret?" He collects his cards.

"Having to leave my family behind in order to save myself, uhh, arguing, and losing friends. I have a lot of regrets," I say sadly. He doesn't say anything, and we move to the next round. This time I have an ace of clubs and he has a two of hearts. "I win, and this is the truth, the worst thing that ever happened to you?" I ask; he shifts uncomfortably in the bed.

"Can you ask a different one? I'll answer that one if you win a war," he suggests; his voice cracks at the end.

"Deal. Biggest fear?" I ask.

"Either losing loved ones or spiders," he answers.

"Spiders? Really?" I joke.

"Yeah, they are creepy," he says. Round three: I put a three of spades and he put a two of diamonds. "That is so not fair," he groans.

"I'ma spice it up. I dare you to take your shirt off and spin," I say. I'm trying to see if he has any scars, bruises, or anything like that. He hesitantly takes his shirt off. "Woah," I whisper. Thankfully, he didn't hear me, but boy, was I right about him having a body. I snap out of it when I see a faint scar across his chest, and when he turns around there are what look like burns. "Where did you get those?" I ask.

"Oh, um, you know—" he starts grumbling up his words.

"The truth, Daniel," I tell him.

"Promise me something first? Promise me that no matter what I tell you, you won't kick me and Jake out?" he asks.

"Of course, Daniel," I blurt out. "That isn't even a question"

"The scar across my chest and the burns were from Robert," he says.

"Woah, Daniel…" I trail off. I fucking knew it.

"Next round, please," he begs, and we flip over the cards; he wins with a queen of clubs. "It's only fair. I dare you to talk your shirt off," he says.

"I hope no one walks in." I laugh. "They might get the wrong idea." I take off my shirt too. I catch him staring, and I snap in front of his face. "Hey, eyes up here," I motion. We move on to the next round, and it's a war between two jacks.

"I…de…clare…war." We flip over the cards, and I win. "Time to answer the question," I tell him.

"I was sexually assaulted by a man," he mumbles. I'm almost not able to even hear what he said. Neither one of us say anything and just move on to the next round. He wins again. "Why do you care so much about me and my brother?" he asks.

"I care because your brother reminds me of mine…. He wasn't the same age, but it just makes me miss him more. You, well…I feel like there is a lot of layers to you, Daniel, and underneath everything, you're very sweet, very kind, and your heart is in the right place, and there aren't many people like you guys anymore. It's refreshing," I tell him.

"Thanks." We both smile. Next round I win again. "I suck at this game." He laughs.

"Is Robert really your dad?" I ask; his whole face drops and all the color fades.

"I-I-I n..no," he stutters out.

"Breathe, Daniel," I say

He takes a deep breath. "No, he was with us on and off for ten years. He was my mom's boyfriend. He isn't Jake's dad either, they were split, and my mom hooked up with my dad again, so don't worry about that. My mom committed suicide, so it was just me and baby Jake with him, and he took advantage of that. He… He was the man who sexually assaulted me," he finishes, and at this point I'm fuming mad. I wanna kill this man.

"I think he assaulted Miko too," I tell Daniel, and he nods shyly.

"I was there. Miko got dropped off at the house. My mom and him were babysitting her. I just stood in my room, minding my business, and I didn't know at first. It was like the third or fourth time she came over, and my mom had to step out to go to the store. I was in the living room playing a video game, and she was in my mom's room watching some stupid cartoon. I heard Robert go in there, and he came out ten minutes later smiling like a real smug douchebag. I peeked inside the room and saw Miko crying. I didn't say anything. It was a young girl crying, I thought she was just having a temper tantrum," he explains. I can see his eyes start to get glossy. "Then one day she just stopped coming, and I guess I know why now. I was only like thirteen, I didn't know. When she left, he started to assault me. I should have put two and two together. God, I was so stupid!" He puts his head in his hands.

I move closer, close enough that our knees were touching. "It's okay, Daniel," I whisper. I gently grab his wrist and move them out of the way. He rests his forehead on mine. Neither one of us say anything for a long time because I just wanted to let him cry it out. This isn't something you interrupt, and especially if you don't know what to do. He started to calm down and leans back slightly. Our faces are only inches apart. "I'm here for you both," I tell him.

"I should have said something, I should have done something," he says; you can hear the guilt in his voice.

"It's okay, Daniel. You didn't know, you were young too," I tell him. Neither one of us say anything anymore and we kind of just stare into each other's eyes. I see the guilt and fear across the glossiness, and I can also see that he keeps glancing at my lips, hoping I'll make the first move. Before, I was always too scared to make the first move for anything at all in the past, but things are different now. I lean in halfway, and he meets me in the middle…. We kiss. At first slow and sweet, almost like out of a really cheesy romantic movie.

We break apart both breathing heavy. "Is this okay?" he asks.

"Daniel, we are just getting to know each other. I don't want to go any further," I tell him truthfully. I don't want my first time to be with someone I'm not with yet.

"That is totally fine by me." He grins.

"I don't think I'm ready for another relationship right now, Daniel," I tell him. I wasn't expecting to kiss him tonight; it was just supposed to be a little game to get him to talk. This is definitely not going to be good. I don't have feelings for him.

"So why did we kiss?" he asks.

"It was a dare. Look, you're nice, and cute, but I can't. I don't see you that way." I can't look him in the eye when saying that.

"Wow." He looks lost. "I better be getting back to my room." He slides off the bed and puts his shirt on quickly. Without another word, he leaves and I lie back sighing heavily.

"Well, that didn't go as planned," I mumble. I try and get some sleep at night, but I didn't for two more reasons than usual: One, Daniel and Two, what he told me.

The morning I wake up by Jake jumping on me. "Weee!"

"Ow, shit." I sit up.

"Miko and Allison said get your ass outside." He giggles.

"Don't curse, whether they tell you or not, understand?" I tell him

"Yes, ma'am." He does a little salute and runs out of the room.

I grab my shirt and put it on. When I get out Allison is playing with Jake, Miko is cooking with Alex…Daniel isn't out yet. I walk up to Allison and Jake. "Stop having the little one curse, be a good influence," I say.

"Sooo bossy." She laughs. "I like it." She raises an eyebrow.

"Yeah, yeah, yeah." I roll my eyes but can't hide the faint smile. Miko seems preoccupied with cooking, but I really do need to talk to her. I walk up and tap her on the shoulder.

"Hey, are you here to lecture me on why I shouldn't be telling Jake to curse?" She laughs but is still looking at the food.

"No, I'm here on a more serious note. We need to talk as soon as breakfast is over. No ifs, ands, or buts," I tell her.

"Uhh, okay then." she seems confused.

"I'm gonna go wake up Daniel." I go to the boys' room and knock.

"Come in," I hear Robert say. I walk in, and Daniel is still sleeping. Robert is tying his shoes. "Good morning, Miranda," he says.

"Hey, look. We were crunching some numbers, and the fact is that food supply is already running short; some of you are gonna need to leave," I start saying.

"Well, then maybe that boy Alex? Or Miko." Is he really trying to give me suggestions?

"And one of those some is you Robert," I tell him.

"Why me?" This time he stands up and stands in front of me. He acts like I'm supposed to be scared of him.

"'Cause you don't do shit," I tell him, looking him dead in the eye.

Daniel wakes up at this point and gets in the middle of the both of us. "What the fuck," he says.

"Your little fucking girlfriend is telling me we have to leave," Robert spats out.

"I said YOU have to leave, not the boys," I tell him.

"Okay, okay. Let's not do or say anything right now, please. Let's just go eat and continue this talk later," Daniel suggests. Robert sucks his teeth and leaves.

"I don't need you to fight my battles, Daniel," I snap at him.

"I'm just trying to keep semi-peace for a little and take some stress off your back," he says.

"Daniel, get over me. We just aren't gonna fit together. It's best for both us and the group if you move on." Without saying anything else, I leave.

"Hey, Miranda! Breakfast is ready!" Miko yells.

"Uh, yeah, I'm not too hungry this morning," I tell her. "Who is lookout?" I ask.

"Alex," Allison says.

Sooner or later, I was gonna have to deal with him anyway. I climb up to the lookout; neither one of us say hi or anything. "I'm sorry for the other day and the food situation. I shouldn't have been like that, but it was just when you said I was banned from hunting. I guess hunting was the one thing I felt like I had a purpose for the group, even though you were good at that too," he finally admits.

"Look, that was the other day, and you are still banned, so don't ask, but I need your help with something more important than that right now," I tell him. "It's about Miko," I say.

"What? What's wrong?" he says, the words practically jumping out his mouth.

"Turns out Robert really did do something to Miko, and I need your help getting rid of him," I tell him.

"I'll kill that sonofabitch." He clenches his jaw.

"Not yet," I try and calm him down. "Here is the plan. I want to kick him out, but it doesn't seem like he is going to go willingly, so I want you, me, Daniel, and Miko to take him out and kill him there. We will tell Jake and Allison that it was an accident, because I don't think it is right for them to know," I explain.

"When?" he asks,

"I still have to tell Miko I know, and I want you to tell Daniel for me, because me and him aren't exactly on speaking terms right now," I say.

"Done and done." He and I shake hands.

"He better enjoy every minute of his morning. Because he isn't going to get anymore after this," I say.

"That was corny, Miranda." Alex rolls his eyes.

"Ugh, you're no fun." I shove him slightly.

Let's hope this plan works...

Alex and I quickly finish our shift and practically jump down the post. "Talk to Daniel, meet me and Miko in front of the gate," I order, and we take off running in different directions. We kind of look like stupid kids, but this is important. "Miko!" I yell; she is standing at the graveyard.

She jumps slightly and turns. "What the hell?" she asks.

I stop short in front of her and take a couple deep breathes. "You… Daniel…Kill…" I breathe out.

"Miranda, just spit it out," she says.

I stand straight and steady my breathing. "I think, Alex is on board. That you and Daniel should kill Robert. Not here! Outside. We make it look like an accident to the others," she looked taken aback for a moment and gains her composer quickly.

"I'm so in," she says; her eyes dilate for a split second.

"Well, Alex is asking Daniel as we speak, so let's go wait by the gate," I tell her. No one is on watch right now until Allison goes; it's really only those two who are the problem.

Miko and I are sitting by the gate. "What is taking them so long?" She sighs, annoyed.

"I don't know." I shrug.

Allison walks up to us with Jake and hands him over. "He is your responsibility now," she says.

"Nope, can't. Miko, Alex, Daniel, and I are gonna take Robert out to learn how to scout, fish, kill, and stuff." I try to sound as calm and convincing as possible.

"I wanna go! I wanna go!" Jake asked.

"No can do, bud, only big kids," I tell him.

"So what do I do with him?" Allison asks.

"Have him go play with something." Miko shrugs them off.

Daniel and Alex come walking with Robert. Miko and I jump up and move over. I guess Alex told him we were going out already. "Yo, let's go," Alex says and opens the gate. I run up next to Alex and stand next to him. "We got somewhere to go, Allison. I got some old toy cars in my room to see. If he gets too annoying, he can play with them. We will be back around dinner," he explains. Without another word, we leave.

"What did you bring?" I whisper over to Alex.

"I got a switchblade, lighter, and matches." He shows me on the side. "Wwhat about you?" he asks.

"I got my gun; obviously, I got my dagger." I show. "I don't know what Daniel brought, but Miko doesn't have anything on her," I say.

"He got rope and tape in his hoodie pocket." Alex motions. "I made him grab it," he tells me. I look back; Daniel and Miko are behind Robert, both with their hands clenched. Daniel sees me looking and looks down.

Once we are a good distance away from the school away from the school, Alex and I stop. The rest fall short and stop. "What are we even doing? I'm an old man. I can't be doing this hunting thing," Robert whines. A grown man whining, what a low life.

"We aren't here to hunt, Robert," Daniel says through clenched teeth.

"What did I say about calling me that in front of people!" Robert yells.

"We know who you really are." I take a step closer.

"Nothing but a pig," Alex spits out and steps closer.

"A pervert." Daniel steps up.

"You got it all wrong, I am a man. We all did things in the past, but this is a chance to start a new life. God forgave Adam and Eve for eating the apple, so forgive me. Yes, I wasn't the best man ever. I never was and never will be a pervert. I have done nothing wrong; this is just a simple misunderstanding." Robert breathes out; he starts to fidget.

"Shut the fuck up!" Miko yells and steps up. "You're nothing but a liar, manipulator, and rapist. You know damn well what you did to me and Daniel. So, for once in your pathetic life, take ownership." Her voice sounds eerily calm. I mean she is obviously mad, you can hear the venom in her voice, but it's in a calm manner. Like scary calm. You see in movies where the killer is explaining how he is gonna kill you, or when someone describes their crime with no remorse.

Alex kicks the back of Robert's leg, making him fall. I cringe slightly remembering my incident. "Tie him up," Alex orders Daniel. Daniel quickly grabs Robert's mouth and covers it with duct tape, then ties his arms around a tree.

"Now which one of you wanna go first?" I ask the two of them. Alex and I lay out the things we have for them to use to get revenge. "The gun is for the very end, when we decide if we let him turn or not." I put the gun down last.

"I'll go first." Miko steps up and grabs the dagger. "If that's okay with you, Daniel," she asks.

"As long as I get a turn, go ahead." Daniel gestures towards Robert.

MIKO'S POV

I take a step closer to Robert, his eyes look like a pleading dog. I grip the handle tighter in my hand. "I want to hear him scream," I say and rip off the tap. He hisses and inhales sharply. I start off small and stab his shoulder. It only makes him wince a little. Next I slice an X across his chest; blood starts dripping on to my hand, and this time he screams bloody murder.

The X it isn't deep enough to kill him fast, but he will definitely faint from the pain in like a good ten minutes. Blood starts trickling from the X at first drips, but it slowly turned into streaks of blood painting over his chest. "Please, I don't want to die," Robert whimpers and begs.

"You don't get to beg or plead anymore, you sonofabitch." I slash the side of his face. Blood splatters across my arm and even a few drops on my face. I dropped the dagger and look at my hands. I should feel bad, and normally, I would. But seeing this, seeing this man suffer for what he did brings more joy than I can even imagine. The blood that is gushing from his cheek, the streaks of blood down his chest, the fact that he can't run, can't move a muscle, shows how I am in control. "Matches," I demanded from Alex; he picks them up and hands them to me.

"Remember I still get a turn," Daniel reminds me.

"After this you can do whatever you want." I waved him off. Robert's breathing is getting heavier; he is trying to suck in enough air.

"Please...do..don't," he breathes out.

Someone places a hand on my shoulder. "We're all in this together," Miranda tells me. She pats my shoulder and steps back.

I flick three matches and press each one into the X marking. "Fucking hell!" Robert yells, his eyes screwed shut. I throw the matches on the ground, step back, and a satisfied smile spreads across my face.

"He is all yours," I tell Daniel.

DANIEL'S POV

"He is all yours," Miko tells me. Now there is only one thing I really want to do.

"I just want to do one thing," I say. I pick up the gun and shoot Robert in the dick.

"Holy…! You…you fu…fucking brat." His heavy breathing starts to pick up even more. The pain and suffering in his voice is actually enjoyable.

"Done," I say. I throw the gun down.

MIRANDA'S POV

"Now what?" I ask Miko and Daniel.

"Let him die. Once he stops breathing, kill him so he doesn't turn," Miko says. Hey eyes are fixed on Robert. I want to stand beside her but I'm afraid she might kill me too.

"Okay," I say. I pick up the gun and hand it to her. "You kill him as soon as he is gone," I tell her. We all watch in silence. Robert's breathing starts to get faint, like he is giving up. He starts coughing up blood; his eyes shut slowly, almost like going to bed.

Alex goes up to the body a few seconds later and checks his pulse. "He's dead," he says.

Miko points the gun at his head and shoots. "Done and done. Now let's go." She hands me back the gun.

"Wait," I say. "We need to get our story straight," I tell everyone.

"She's right. Miko, you're covered with blood, and there is no way we can go back empty handed," Alex says.

Miko takes a quick glance at her hands. "I'll clean up at the river. Daniel can come with me and get some fish, and you two could hunt around for something," she suggests.

"That's not a bad idea. We meet back here as soon as possible, understand?" I tell everyone; they all just nod. "Move your asses," I shoo them all, and they finally move.

"We can tell the others that we got attacked and Robert told us to run," Alex says.

"Just leave the talking to me," I tell him. "Now let's see if we can find a raccoon, rabbit, or something." We start searching.

"Anyway, look." I point. There was a rabbit. "Honestly, I don't care right now." I pulled out my gun and shoot the rabbit. I point and Alex just stares at me. "Come on, don't make me get it," I whine.

"Ugh, fine." He picks it up and put it over his shoulder. We walk back to Robert's body and the other two are already waiting for us.

"Took you two long enough," Miko says.

"Let's just get back to the school." I roll my eyes and take off walking.

Daniel runs up next to me. "So um…" He trails off.

"Daniel, stop. I know it's weird, but it was just a kiss. Yes, it was cute, but I really don't see you like that." I lower my voice so only he hears.

"Oh, okay," he whispers back and trails behind me.

This isn't something anyone needs right now. No more relationships, at least for the moment. We reach the school. I look up and Allison is on watch. "We need to talk!" I yell up, catching her attention.

"I can hear you!" she yells back.

Jake comes running up to us as we enter the school. "Where is Robert?" he asks frantically. Is he scared he will come back, or did he actually care for this man?

I look back at the others and look at Jake "That's what we need to talk about." I take a deep breath, rethinking what I'm about to say. "We went fishing first, but we wanted to make sure we had enough food for tonight and even the next, so we went hunting. We got swarmed, Robert told us to leave, and he would fend them off. We took off running…none of us looked back, afraid of what we might have saw," I explain.

Allison just looks down at us, shocked.

"So no more Daddy?" Jake asked.

"You don't have to call him that anymore, bud," Daniel tells Jake.

"Okay, one, what do you mean by that, Daniel? And two, are you guys okay?" Allison asks; her eyes glance over all of us as she slowly makes her way down the ladder.

"One, don't worry about it, and two, we are all okay, I promise," I try and comfort and convince her. Allison still looks a little skeptical, but she doesn't speak about what is on her mind,

"I…I think I should leave," Daniel blurts out. This time it's Miko and my turn to be shocked. "Why?" I ask.

"There is just, I don't, it's not." He looks lost, like he is trying to gather his thoughts together.

"You know what, you wanna go, go then." I shrug. His eyes go wide, fear flashes in them. Well, if he didn't want to go then why did he say so? Of course I don't want him to leave, but I won't force him to stay.

"Alrighty." He clears his throat.

"Miranda, don't you think you're being harsh?" Allison asks.

"Hey! It's not for us to speak about, Allison. We should stay out of it," Miko chimes in.

"Come on, Jake!" Daniel yells up. Jake is up with Alex on watch.

"Oh, no, Jake stays here," I tell him.

"He is my brother," Daniel says.

"But I won't put a child in danger," I snap back. Now I'm starting to get annoyed. Like, you just pop up with wanting to leave out of nowhere and now want to take a child too? Nope not on my watch.

"I don't wanna leave!" Jake whines and hide behind Allison.

"There you go, he doesn't wanna leave," I tell him

"Miranda!" Allison shouts.

"Allison, stop," Miko says.

"Fine, Jake, stay with these people! I'm… I don't want to be here. I just don't think it's right, guys. After today I won't feel right here. Knowing that I helped. Maybe I'm weak, but then but I want to start fresh, with a group that never had Robert in it," Daniel explains. He actually makes sense this time around.

I sigh. "Okay, but here." I hand Daniel Kev's old gun, and it's completely loaded. I also hand them two waters and two cans of food.

"Thank you," Daniel says.

"Be careful." Allison hugs him tightly.

"See you, man." Alex fist-bumps him.

"Bye." Miko waves.

Daniel kneels down to Jake's level. "I'm gonna miss you so much, little bro, but I know you're in good hands. I trust Miranda even if I said I didn't. Be a good little boy and listen to them, okay? I'll come back and visit as much as I can." Daniel and Jake both start to tear up. Daniel gives Jake a coin and hugs him tightly. "I love you," Daniel chokes out.

"I love you too." Jake lets go and wipes his nose with Miko's hand.

"Ew, you nasty little sh—" Miko starts.

"No," I tell her, holding back my laugh as she flips me off. Daniel stands up and faces me. "It was a pleasure." I give him a handshake. "Alex, lock the gate once he leave," I tell him, and he walks them to the gate. The four of us watch as Daniel leaves, and Alex slowly closes the gate and locks it.

Nothing is forever

Once he is fully out of everyone's view, I turn to the group. "Even though this is sad we still have stuff we need to do. For example, starting tomorrow morning Miko and I will be training Jake with weapons and hand-to-hand combat. Alex will be teaching Jake watch duty rules, Allison, you want to be his babysitter when the three of us go our way? And he is to learn how to cook by helping you," I tell everyone.

"Wait, what? Why do I have to help? Alex is better with weapons anyway!" Miko exaggerates.

"Yes, I know he is better with a GUN, but I am not letting a seven-year-old hold a gun, so you will be teaching him melee combat weapons," I tell her.

"BUT WHY!?" she yells.

"First, don't yell, and second, we are teaching him hand-to-hand and melee," I tell her.

"But—" I cut her off. Feels good to cut people off, no wonder Allison does it all the time.

"End. Of. Discussion," I say seriously; she doesn't say anything. Instead, she storms off.

Allison comes to me and hugs me. "You can't always make everyone happy. You did well stating your authority, Miranda. Don't worry about Miko." She pats my back and walks off.

Alex side-hugs me. "She is probably just upset because he left." He leaves to do his own training. Jake is just standing there, not moving, staring at this coin. I don't understand why it is so important. I never heard Daniel talk about it or even seen it before.

I kneel down to Jake's height. "Hey, how you feeling?" I ask and place a hand on his shoulder.

"I'm really sad. I lost everyone. My brother left; did he not love me?" He tears up again.

"Hey, little man. He left because he loved you too much. He didn't want to hurt you." As I say those words I finally think I know the real reason Miko doesn't wanna be around Jake and why Daniel left....

"But isn't Daddy out there. He hurt Daniel," Jake says.

"Daniel isn't gonna get hurt by Robert anymore, okay? I promise." I hold out my pinky and he links his pinky. "Now, why is that coin special?" I ask.

"Daniel said when Mommy died and then our new daddy showed up that this was in Mommy's pocket. It's a quarter, see!" He shows me the coin, and it was definitely just a quarter. "We didn't have much from Mommy. Daniel had this quarter and a picture of Mommy," he says.

"Aww, that's cute." I smile. Jake hugs me. "Okay, well, it's getting late, you should probably go to bed in your room," I tell him.

"It all mine!" he asked excitedly, and I nod. "Cool!" He runs to the rooms, and I sigh and sit on the floor.

I run my hands through my hair and sigh heavily. It's like there is no family anymore. I guess it's just hard to have a family when so many members are gone. We are hanging by a thread more than ever before, and it doesn't look good for us. I mean how are you supposed to remain positive in a damn apocalypse? I used to say nothing was impossible, but now I think it's impossible for us to get back to before and impossible to be truly happy during this time. It really might be easier to just die than keep fighting and die later. I pick up a rock and toss it between both hands. "Fuck this," I whisper and throw the rock away. I stand up and go to my room and stand in the middle. I look over to the box where all my family pictures and memories are and sit next to it. I dig into the box and pull out my brother's toy; he was always into sooo many different things. I put it back immediately and sit on my bed. It's always so quiet, it's not hard to slip into the mindset I'm in right now. And ever since that incident with Kevin, this mindset is all I slip into. I decide to try and get some sleep.

I wake up to Jake sitting on my bed poking me. "Wakey wakey." He giggles.

"What do you want, Jake?" I sit up and rub my eyes.

"Allison said to wake you up 'cause breakfast's ready," he says.

"Okay, I'm coming." I get up fully and throw on a hat. Jake and I walk out, and everyone is eating.

I grab some granola and blueberries. "Good morning," everyone says.

"Morning, guys." I half smile and sit down to eat. We eat, and the conversation is a minimally adequate convo about the damn weather. I finish first, which makes no sense because I was the last one to start eating but whatever. "Jake and Miko, meet me in the sparing ground as soon as you guys are done," I tell them both.

As soon as I get to the ground, Jake is running up to me. "I done! Miko said give her five minutes!" he says.

"Well, that means me and you can start first. Put your fist up like this." I put my fist up evenly up to my face. "And whatever you do, never put your hands down." I tell him seriously. He puts his fist up just like mine. "Now your left hand, hit my right hand, and your right hand hit my left hand, got it?" He nods excitedly and starts hitting my hands. He does it about five times. "Good, good, stop." I put my hands down, and Miko finally shows up. "That was a long ass five minutes," I joke.

"Sorry." She fake smiles, like I can't tell she is faking.

"Just for you being rude this morning, I'm gonna sit on the side and let you do all the teaching," I say with a smirk. Her eyes go slightly bigger, then narrow with anger, and I smile. "Here, you are gonna start him with this." I hand her a slightly sharpened butter knife; it technically can't cut through anything yet, but it's good to get a feeling of slashing a weapon in your hand before you start with the weapons.

"Okay, Jake…um here." She hands it to him.

"Ooh, cool. Do I get to go around stabbing things!" he says.

"Not yet, bud, soon," she says. See, she has a soft side saying "bud," but if I tell her that now that she is finally out of that other phase when this all started, she might hurt me. "So, I want you to run to that tree and stab it." She points to a small target.

After a more or less ten minutes, I got super bored watching them, so I walk away. I went up to Alex, who is still on watch duty every day and just about every night. "Hey," I say.

"Shouldn't you be downstairs teaching Jake?" he answers back, not taking his eyes off the horizon.

"Miko is doing that right now. How long has it been since you slept?" I ask.

"I slept last night. Allison couldn't sleep so she offered to stay up and do the night shift; she does it from time to time," he says, side-eyeing me. Allison has been having trouble sleeping? Why wasn't she telling me that?

"Do you wanna take a break now?" I ask.

"Miranda…when will I be able to hunt again?" He completely ignores my question and I stare back, dumbfounded. Before I can speak, he starts talking again. "This isn't my full potential, we all know this. I should be out there with the gun, not just holding it in my lap and watching. It's not fair," he rants.

"You're right. I guess things have just been shaky since what we did to Robert and then people leaving again. Just give it time, you will be back soon," I tell him. It doesn't seem to ease him at all. He goes back to ignoring me and I just go back down. Allison is having another hard time? I think it's best if I let this one go, or have her come up to me. I'm gonna talk about how Miko and Allison feel about having Alex back on hunting. I think it's time. We all been avoiding it, and I can see it eating away at him.

"Ugh! Miranda, can you come over here!" Miko yells.

"Yes?" Jake is sitting at the tree. Crying. "What the hell did you do?" I ask.

"I didn't do anything! I told the kid to relax because he wasn't listening. He told me to leave him alone, so I said maybe because he is so goddamn annoying that's why his brother left and now he is crying. He is being way too sensitive right now and I don't know what to do. Help," she explains and points to the kid.

"I'm not good with kids, but I'll try." I roll my eyes. "Just for that, the first time Alex goes fishing, you and Jake can go," I say.

"You're letting him hunt again?" she says, surprised.

"I'm thinking about it. If it was you, I know you would get bored doing the same thing twenty-four seven, and it isn't even something you enjoy," I try to explain. I hear Jake whimper. "Okay, little guy." I pick him up.

"But why with me? Of all people?" she says.

"Because like it or not we are a family that has to coexist. It's not my fault you guys decided to do what you did. Now live with the consequences. Now excuse me but I have to take care of a crying kid." I sigh and walk past her.

"Hey! Is he okay?" Alex yells from on top of the lookout.

"Yeah, just upset. Why?" I ask.

"I uh, nothing, just heard him crying." He shrugs it off.

"Alex, come down!" I yell up to him; once he is down, I hand Jake to him. "You're the only guy here, he just lost his brother, I think it's best if you take him to his room and try to cheer him up," I explain.

"Okaaaaay, I'll try." Alex gives me a reassuring nod.

"Miko!" I yell.

"WHAT!"

"You're on guard duty!" I hear her groan. "Hurry your ass!" I yell.

"I'm coming, I'm coming!" she yells, running up to me. "You get on my nerves," she says,

"Ha…ha…ha…you're so funny. I can see you trying to hold back from laughing. And it's okay, you get on my nerves too." I smile and nudge past her while she gets to her post. "Now don't let us die!"

"I make no promises."

ALEX'S POV

I don't know why Mirada wants me to help Jake, I never had siblings. When I enter Jake's room, I see him crying in bed holding that coin his brother gave him. "Hey, Jake," I say warmly.

He looks up and wipes his tears. "Hello" he sniffles.

"I heard you weren't happy, so I figured we could play with toys? I got my cars." I pull out the toy cars I still have. All of us have at least one sentimental item from the past I think. I know me, Miko, and Miranda do.

"R-really?" he says.

"Yep," I say and sit on his floor. "Come on, I can't sit here all dayyyyy," I exaggerate.

Jake giggles and sits next to me. "I want that one." He points. "Uhh hey, why you got that long scratch on your arm?" Jake points to my right arm.

"Oh, uh, I got into a fight. Don't worry, it doesn't hurt." I shake it off. Damn…it is slower than it used to be. Maybe that's why Miranda doesn't want me out.

"That's a big owie, but I wanna play!" he squeals.

"Here now, let's race!" I say.

Maybe I'm not too bad with kids.

MIKO'S POV

I hate keeping watch! No wonder Alex was going crazy here, this is so boring. I almost never watch because I'm cooking or even hunting. Maybe I should go apologize to Jake. Or I could torment him? Or at the very least see if he still wants to train with me. "Miranda!" I yell and look back; she isn't there. Must have gone looking for Allison. I doubt five minutes of no one on watch will be fine. I mean we have done it before. "But we are always outside," I whisper. "Fuck it, I'll be right back," I say to myself and jump down.

ALLISON'S POV

I'm in my room alone, again. It's honestly my fault because I've just been feeling off. I haven't been talking much to anyone recently, and I don't know why. I've been looking over old photos and items and it just made me realize everybody we lost so far. We lost…so many people. We were all supposed to live, to make it out of this hellhole. Maybe the only way to survive this is to adapt to it. I'm getting tired of just surviving. I'm losing everyone, both physically and emotionally. Jake is the future, and I understand that, but it's not fair that he is being destroyed and this ball of sunshine doesn't have any harm to him. Am I even listening to myself? Am I really jealous over a little boy? Yeah, I guess I am. I grabbed a razor blade and fiddle with it in my fingers. Who am I becoming?

MIRANDA'S POV

I'm on my way to talk to Allison to see if she how she feels about Alex going back on hunting duties. I knock on her door. "Who is it?" she says.

"Miranda," I shout back. When there is no response, I assume I can come in, so I open the door slowly. I thought I heard something slide across her floor, but when I opened the door fully, I didn't see anything. "Is everything okay?" I look around the room.

"Yeah, just feel a little down I guess." She shrugs off.

I sit next to her. "Well, talk to me." I see her eyes shift and quickly look somewhere; it looks like either towards her nightstand or the bed.

"I don't feel like talking," she says. "Now leave." she gestures to the door.

"Are you—"

"Yes," she says firmly, cutting me off. I get up to leave without another word. "I'm sorry," she says softly as I close the door behind me. Once I turn around, I bump into Miko.

"Miko, what the hell? You should be on watch!" I whisper/yell at her.

She looks at me wide-eyed. "I went to uh, apologize to Jake," she says.

"Bullshit, come with me." I nudge her shoulder to the door. "If you really wanna apologize it can wait until he has his shift with me," I explain.

We get outside and I do a scan of the outside. "See, nothing five minutes didn't kill," she sighs out.

"Miko, what's that then?" I point directly in front of our gate. I run up to grab it. "It looks like a note, fucking great." I open up the note for it to say.

"We are here." Who the hell is still here? I thought any problems we had were gone. I feel Miko trying to read over my shoulder. Key word is trying, she's too short to see.

"I wanna see." She goes on her tiptoes.

"Maybe if you actually were at your post you would have seen it already," I scoff and show her.

She raises an eyebrow while she reads. "This doesn't sound right; we should tell the others," she tells me.

"You're right, go tell everyone to come out here right now. Urgent meeting." I stand on the table as she runs off to tell everyone. "Fucking hell." I sigh, annoyed, and look back to the gravesite. I'm not ready to lose any more people. I look out to the gates: whoever this is I hope knows what is in store.

A few seconds later everyone comes out the school and stands facing me. "Everyone is here," Miko says, I guess she is trying to make up for leaving her post.

"I'm gonna start by saying this: Miko is no longer allowed to be on watch on her own, either Jake, Allison, or myself must assist her." Miko rolls her eyes as I continue to explain. "Secondly, we have received a note saying 'We are here.' I don't know who wrote it or how big of a threat they are. But this is to be taken extremely seriously; everyone must carry their guns at all time. Jake, you will have to constantly be with one of us, and please take watch seriously. We need to make sure we catch whoever comes back," I finish, and everyone takes a second to process the information.

"Are you sure this is a threat?" Allison asks.

"Honestly, I'm not sure of anything right now about this. But it's better to be safe than sorry and take the safety steps," I answer. Do I think sleeping with a gun under your pillow or beside you in bed is a good idea? Not at all. Am I gonna say that? Nope, because I'm gonna do it too.

Jake raises his hand to say something, and I point to him and nod. "Um, what if it is my brother who wrote the note? To let me know he safe!" Jake has a hopeful smile on his face.

"Yeah, it could just be a sign that he is still alive," Alex points out.

"Yeah…yeah that isn't such a bad idea either. I still want everyone to do what I said. But keep in mind it could mean that too. You guys are dismissed," I say as everyone walks off. I hop off the table and go take my turn as look out. The sun is setting. They made a unanimous vote that I am not allowed to stay on watch past sunset because then I will stay here all night, every night. So instead, Allison, then Alex takes turns at night. I can't believe I didn't think it could have been Daniel trying to tell his little brother he was okay. I hope that's what it was; only time will tell at this point. I look down and see three zombies roaming around. This isn't a big deal; our max allowed to be seen is ten. Anything past that we try killing them; if it's a herd we make sure the gates are closed and we all are in our rooms not saying a word or moving a muscle. We have only encountered one pretty big herd, thankfully. But I try to just watch the sunset without thinking on what could happen next.

The sun has fully gone down, and it is almost pitch black when I hear "pssst" being whispered from below me. I look down. "It's my turn, go head up to bed." Allison waves.

"I'm not tired yet," I whisper back.

"Come on, we all decided it was a good idea for you not to stay up all night long here." She sighs. "You come down or I go up," she says.

"Fine." I roll my eyes and come down the ladder. We say our goodnights and I head off to my room. When I'm in the hall, I see Alex walking out of Jake's room. "What are you doing?" I ask.

He jumps a little as if I startled him. "Jake wanted me to tell him a story before bed," he smiles as he speaks.

"I'm glad you're bonding with him; maybe you can help me with having Miko adjust to living with a child," I suggest; he looks hesitant at first.

"Um, maybe, I'll put a pin in that," he says, and he walks away. I go to my room and go straight to my bed and try to fall asleep. I wake up, grab my gun and dagger again, since I'm going hunting and salvage other places today.

Once breakfast is done, everyone is having a small side conversation. I clear my throat, but no one hears. "Hey!" I shout, and everyone stops talking. "Great, now that everyone is paying attention, Allison, you take Jake to the garden and check on crops we are running low. Miko, you're with me; we need to find more medicine. After all the things that have been happening all the medicine and bandages are almost depleted." Before I finish Allison cuts me off….

"Isn't the house far away? And that's like the only house?" she asks.

"Okay, as I was GOING to say, the house that we use to take from is empty from the last event, but as of right now we don't really know if there is nothing else left out there, so I was thinking we walk to the house, stay the night, and walk more in the morning. I know we all remember all the stores and gas stations we passed only about three miles past that house. The house will now be a safehouse we use for long travels," I state.

Alex sighs loudly. "I'm not going again!?" he raises his voice slightly

"Lower your tone. I told you when I thought you were ready," I tell him.

"No!" He slams his hands on the table and stands. "This is bullshit! You know what." He throws his gun on the table. "If I can't go out with it, then I don't want it." He walks away and heads straight for the dorms.

"Does Alex need a hug?" Jake says quietly.

Allison takes Jake's hand. "No, buddy, but I need your help in the garden." Allison looks at me. "You're doing the right thing. If you guys are leaving soon, grab some food from the garden before you go." She smiles slightly and takes Jake away.

Miko picks up Alex's gun, "If he doesn't want it, can I—"

"No," I cut her off and take the gun away. "Pack a small bag. We leave after the garden with Allison; pack ammo, weapons, and anything else. This might be like a three-day trip," I tell her.

"Fuck." She groans and walks off. I go to my room and grab a bag from the closet. I put on my favorite cap and pack a bunch of ammo and go to the nurse's room for the last of the bandages, matches, one of the last three bottles of painkillers, a bottle of anti-biotics, a bottle of peroxide, and needle and thread.

"Hope we find supplies, because if we use this shit we are fucked," I whisper to myself. I'm only packing this stuff because I know how accident prone I am, and even Miko sometimes. "One more thing to do before the garden." I pull Alex's gun out and go knock on his door. I hear a very firm "Go away," but I bang louder, then I hear a loud groan and he opens the door.

"Stop being an asshole." I shove the gun to him. "Take your gun, watch out for Allison and Jake; nothing happens or goes wrong, then you can go hunting again. Let me be clear, you are NOT in charge, Allison is, but you're the best and only protection they have. So if you really give a damn about ever going hunting again, better yet if you care for Jake, you will suck it up and stop winning," I rant, and he looks at me, a little taken aback.

"Uh, yeah… Yeah, sure." He nods. "You and Miko have a safe trip." He closes his door, and as I walk down the hall, Miko comes out of her room with her bag and her bow and arrow on her back.

"Let's go get some food from Allison before we leave," I tell her, and we walk over in silence to the garden.

"We have to be careful," as we get closer Miko states out of nowhere.

"I don't think Jake and Allison are gonna attack us." I chuckle, but Miko is stone-faced.

"That's not what I meant." She stops short and turns to me. "This trip, it's not the first time we been out this far, but last time we did we had a car, so that was a long time ago, at least six months ago, a lot has changed probably since then, Miranda. And I ain't saying that I'm scared, I'm saying we need to be cautious," she explains.

I nodded and put a hand on her shoulder. "I know, but we had a ton of supplies from the school and even some from the house. We are running out. I basically took almost all of the supplies for this trip of ours, and we barely have any. I know we have to be careful. I promise you, we will be. Now, food, before we starve." I laugh and walk past her, and she follows.

Jake runs up to me and hugs me. "I've been gardening." He giggles.

"Good job." I ruffle his hair.

"We are burning daylight. Jake, is Allison ready with any of the food she said she was gonna pack?" Miko asks.

"Mhm! There! She's there!" he points to the greenhouse.

"I'll get the food," I tell her.

"Tell her bye for me!" she shouts behind me as I enter the greenhouse.

Allison turns around when the door creaks open "Hey, food is in the bag; it has four water bottles, a couple of canned peaches, and the rest of the rice we stashed away. I also packed two cans of beans. Please get any protein bars, cans, seeds…anything." She looks worried, worried about us leaving, and worried about us being gone.

"Miko says goodbye, and we will be okay," I tell her, and we hug goodbye. *…Stay down, stay hidden, stay alive…*

Miko and I make it to the house. "Check the floors first," I tell her.

"Can we do it together. When we split up it doesn't end well." Miko takes a step closer next to me.

"Yeah, we check the basement first and work our way up, at least we know there is a bed here." I shrug. "Which I'm obviously taking." I laugh, and she gives me a glare.

"Yeah, okay." She rolls her eyes. We check around the house first and I spot one walking alone. I signal Miko to be quiet, and I sneak up and stab him right in the back of his head. When I pull the blade out, blood splatters across my face. "Ew." Miko fake gags.

I cringe and turn around slowly. "This is so nasty; please use a little water and clean this off," I ask.

"Hmm." The corner of her mouth turns into a smirk. "I'll help you get it off, if I can get the bed," she says.

"You're evil." I groan and huff. "Just get it out he bag and help me, take the bed, I don't care." I roll my eyes.

She laughs and grabs the bottle and cleans off the blood. "There, you big baby." She laughs more.

"You know what…" I grab the bottle and throw water on her and close the bottle. She gasps and jumps back.

"Okay, one, you are an asshole and two, not a good idea dumbass wasting water," she says.

"Wellllllll, worth it." I chuckle. "Come on, let's finish." We check the other floors, but everything else was clear. We sit in the master bedroom, the only room with the bed still there, and eat some peaches.

"Tomorrow we definitely need to hunt," she says, and I nod in agreement. We finish eating and sat there in silence, which feels like an hour but I think it was only twenty minutes. "We aren't gonna just sit here until we go to sleep, then not talk more in the morning?" She laughs slightly.

"Well, what do you wanna talk about?" I ask, and she shrugs. "Great, so much help." I roll my eyes and laugh. "How about what do you think you will be doing in the old world, if this never happened?" I ask.

"If the old world was still a reality, I hopefully would be in college, freshman year." She sighs.

"What would you study?" I ask.

She takes a deep breath and a long sigh. "Okay, so I have so many ideas, like five, but if I had to limit to two, I'd probably major in psychology and minor in English. What about you?" She breaks into a small smile, probably daydreaming about being a lawyer or a writer.

"Theater, I would definitely major in theater and minor in photography maybe. I don't know about a minor." I shrug.

"You remember when Allison lost one of the props for set?" Miko chuckles.

"Ohhhh yeah, Mr. Lin flipped out! Just to find out that Victoria had it." We both laugh harder. We spend the rest of the night rethinking our short-lived high school experience and our hope for a life after this.

I wake up after falling asleep in a wooden chair with a stiff neck and my back slightly aching. "How did you sleep?" I hear Miko ask as I stand to try and stretch.

"Like shit, my back and neck hurts," I whine.

"That sucks, I slept—"

"If you tell me you slept good I will push you into a zombie." I glare, and she laughs.

"Ouch, come on, the sooner we are there, the sooner we can come back and then go home," she says, and we pick up our things and set out walking through the forest. We were walking for at least an hour, and we haven't seen anything but trees and the casual zombie or two. Thankfully there aren't more than three at a time, so we are able to take them out without wasting ammo.

"Wait, my feet are killing me," I say, and we sit on a nearby rock to catch our breath and drink some water.

"I really, really hope we find something and this journey isn't for nothing," she says.

"I mean, we can only hope. We haven't had a car for eight months, so we haven't been this far out in almost a year. It's dangerous, and a low percent of finding anything, but we have gotten to the point that a low percent is better than a zero percent," I try to explain. If you would have asked thirteen-year-old me to have faith and hope in something, I would have laughed but now, having hope is what keeps anyone alive anymore; it's the only thing besides breathing that really separates us between the walking dead.

"Come on, let's keep going," Miko says and gets up.

"Ughhh." I don't move.

"Let's go." She grabs my wrist and pulls me up. I leave an empty water bottle and an old can of food by the rock, so when we walk back we will know we are going the right way. We walk a little faster for another forty minutes "Yo, look." Miko points in the distance.

"Looks like it's a gas station." I look closer. "Yeah, definitely." I nod in confirmation.

"Good, let's hope it hasn't been cleaned out yet," she says hopefully.

Once we get to the gas station, it reeks of death. It gets a lot stronger the closer we get; we stop ten feet away, and we both start gagging. "God, what the hell happened here?" I say and cover my mouth and nose.

"I…I don't, don't know" Miko says in between gages.

"Looks like they got surrounded and were outnumbered." We look around and there are a ton of dead survivors, and zombies are dead all around; blood is everywhere. It looks like a scene from a movie. "We should probably check the pockets of the survivors," I tell her.

"Uhhh, why do you want to check the dead corpses?" she asks.

"Well, they died fighting zombies, and since it looks like they only lost because they were outnumbered, then they didn't plan to die, right?" I ask; she nods hesitantly. "So they might have things still on them that might help us, guns, ammo, food, medicine, we don't know. So how about you take the ones by the pumps, and I'll look at the ones in front of the store," I point and tell her. "Just be careful," I say.

"Obviously, but yeah, you too." We go our separate ways.

I sneak up on one of the corpses and check the pockets of this guy. "Come on, man, have something," I whisper, and pull out a pocketknife and three bullets. "Better than nothin'" I shrug and put the stuff in my bag. We both finished checking; she found someone's gun, with half a clip in it. "All right, we gotta go in there." I try to pull and push the door, but it doesn't budge.

"It's locked," she says.

"Nooooo," I say sarcastically and motion for her to stand back. I take a step back and kick the door. *Once, twice, third* time it bursts open. We both start grabbing anything we find, batteries, food, toiletries. "We hit the jackpot." I laugh, but she doesn't.

"I know this is great, but let's just be in and out, 'cause besides that smell outside, this place is too loaded for me. It never should be this easy," she warns.

"Maybe we caught a break? Don't you think we deserve one?" I ask.

"That's not what I'm saying, we are all in this predicament, some worse than us. So, actually, don't we all need a break?" she asks back.

I sigh. "You're killing my mood." I roll my eyes. "Look." I point to the pharmacy, gated.

"We definitely need to go in there," she says.

"I know." I try to pull on the gate, and it lifts a little. "Come help." We both pull as hard and as much as we can and we get it about two to three feet off the ground. I squat down, and we both slide inside. I go to one of the shelves, stick my arm out, and just sweep all the meds in my bag. "I'm full," I tell her.

"Me too." She nods and we duck back and slide back under the gate. "Great, we crash one more day at the house." She sighs in relief. When we walk out, we are still talking. "I can't wait for Allison to use some of the new spic—" Miko gets cut off by a gunshot grazing past us.

We both freeze. "Hands behind your fucking head! Down on the ground!" a man with a bandana around his mouth demands. There are four of them, two guys and two girls. Fuck… more raiders. Only two are wearing bandanas, one of the guys and one of the girls. The guy with the bandana has dark black eyes and is like six feet tall, and has a tattoo of a shark on his hand; another guy has a regular green cap and looks like he doesn't wanna be there; the first one looks stone-faced. I don't even think he has blinked, and his face is as straight as a line, and his dark brown eyes look almost black and lifeless. Just looking at him makes the hairs on my neck stand up. The girl with a bandana around her mouth is a blonde, with green eyes, and the other girl is definitely Hispanic, brown eyes, jet-black hair, and caramel skin.

"Hey, look, you can take—" I try to rationalize, but the blond girl shoots me in the shoulder; a strong zinging pain goes up and down my entire arm. I clench my shoulder and drop on my knees, blood seeping through my fingertips. "Ah! Fuck... Fuck," I hiss out in pain and breathe heavy.

"Miranda!" Miko tries to go to me, but the guy who yelled at us puts a gun right in front of her.

"Yo what the fuck?" the Hispanic girl yells and puts her hand over my shoulder. "The fuck you going around shooting! Every zombie for god knows how far could have heard it, plus we are wasting bullets and our fucking supply. Now we gotta patch her up, dumbass!" she yells.

"We could just leave them and take their shit," the other guy suggests as he starts collecting everything we got.

"Why are you guys doing this?" Miko asks. "She already said you could take it!" she raises her voice, clearly annoyed.

I try to stand but start to feel a little dizzy and stumble slightly, but the girl catches me. "Hey, it's okay, sit." She helps me sit upside the house and takes my gun. "Sorry, protection," and places it in her back pocket and goes back to applying pressure.

"We don't have time for this shit," the blond girl says. "Are we leaving this one and just taking the other one, or what? The longer we stay here the worse—" she says, irritated.

"Don't...Don't leave me...here." I breathe out. "Don't let...let me turn." I gulp and groan in pain.

"You." The Hispanic girl points to Miko. "You keep applying pressure to your friend's wound, I'll help her walk." She helps me stand, and the guy allows Miko run over to help. "If you guys are so nervous about them, take the other one's gun and hold a gun on her, but we are leaving now," she demands. I guess she is the leader.... If not, she should be.

"Ca....can," I try to speak, but she cuts me off.

"Save your strength for walking instead of talking. We will answer questions later"

I don't remember much of the walk, after what the girl said. When I come too again, I'm handcuffed by my left wrist to a bedpost in what looks like a little cabin, definitely not in the house or by the school anymore. We got caught; it took us this long. After all this just to get caught by a group of people who don't look much older than us. "I need to get out of here," I whisper and look around the room. "Fuck, nothing." There is literally only a window, a small table, and a bed.

A few seconds later a guy walks in with scrubs and gloves and with a name tag that said Tyler on it. "You're up? Good, you have been out for hours," he says.

"How long have I been out?" I ask. I need to get to Miko, make sure she is okay, like hours ago.

"Five hours total. You need to be seen by the leaders of the town first." Town? Where the fuck am I?

"Where is my partner!" I try to sit up but fail.

"Oh yeah." He stands and unlocks the cuffs. "I'm supposed to wait here—" He is dodging my question, so I cut him off.

"Where. Is. My. Partner?" I demand and clench my fist. He pulls out a gun and places it on his lap, and I tense slightly.

"I don't want to have to do this. I think you're a good person. But don't make me have to shoot you because you wanna be stupid. She's fine." He rolls his eyes.

Fine? Fine could mean anything… He knows that. He wants me to be on my guard, to be anxious. "Can I at least stand up and stretch?" I ask, and he shrugs, and I roll my eyes and stand up and crack my knuckles and back. I look out the window and see another little cabin off to the right slightly and an abandoned four-story little building off to the left. Guess that's what he meant by town. It would be really nice if I knew exactly when these people are coming, or at least how many leaders there are. The room is so dirty; there is dry blood splatter on one of the walls and some on the floor. *Something bad happened here, and by the looks of it really recently 'cause the blood looks like it just dried*, I thought. My stomach kind of twisted at the split thought that it could have been Miko.

There was a knock on the door a little while later. I didn't turn to face them at first and I took a deep breath. "Turn around!" a male voice shouts. I turn around slowly and see four people, two of them. There is the Hispanic girl and the guy with the shark tattoo, then there is a new girl, dark skin, with curly black hair. When I do a quick scan, my eyes go wide. Daniel… he's one of the leaders!?

I see his eyes widen for a second too. He clears his throat before he speaks. "Tyler, step out," Daniel orders, and the doctor runs out like he is scared of Daniel, Daniel…really? "What's your name, where are you from, who is the girl—" he starts listing questions with a stone-cold monotone voice.

"I won't remember all the questions if you give them all at once," I say sarcastically. "How about I just give you my background check, you guys give me my friend and some answers, and I'll be on my way. You will never hear from me again. I swear." I put my hand up and cross my heart with a sly smirk on my face. Whatever they are about to ask or do to me, I might as well have some fun first. I see the other guy roll his eyes, but before any of them can speak again, I start, "My name is Miranda. My friend? Her name is Miko, it's only us now. The rest of our people died after we ran out of supplies." I tell the story stoneface, and when I say everyone died I see Daniel catch his breath, worried about Jake I assume.

"We still need to know more about you," the second guy demands.

"Not until I at least find out who you guys are, and where's my friend?" I shoot back; the guy chuckles and grins. *Oh, how I wish I could bash his head in right now*

"That's not how it works—" he starts, but Daniel cuts him off.

"My name is Daniel," he introduces himself.

"Destiny," the dark-skinned girl says.

"Ryder," Mr. Wanna-be Bad Shark Tattoo Asshole says.

"Claire," the Hispanic girl finishes her name.

"Now, my friend," I insist.

"She's safe, she's locked away right now because when they tried to question her, she hit one of our guys," Claire starts explaining. I let out a small laugh but try to disguise it as a cough. "You'll be joining her soon, after we are finished," she says.

"I only want to talk to Claire. Sorry, Destiny, I don't know who you are. Daniel can stay I guess, if you don't want to be alone, but I won't speak if this asshole is standing in front of me." I spit down at Ryder's shoes; this guy gets no respect from me.

He tries to step to me, but Claire straight-arms his chest. She looks at me and back at the rest of the leaders. She's smart enough to know I'm not joking, but as a leader you never want to give in right away to someone you don't trust. I hate being in her shoes; in a weird way it's nice being on the other side. You know, without the whole possibility I could die. "Fine, ALL of you step out. This will only take a minute and I will call for you if I need help," she tells them. Ryder stares me up and down before sucking his teeth and walking outside.

"We will be right down the hall; don't hesitate to get us," Destiny tells Claire.

Daniel doesn't say anything at first. As he starts to walk out the room, he looks back at me, then at Claire and says, "Find out everything you can." She nods, and he shuts the door behind him.

No one says anything for a few seconds, and I start to feel a sharp pain all over my shoulder and down my arm, so I sit down and take medicine I see on the desk. "How's that by the way?" she asks. I guess that's the best way to break the awkwardness.

"Hurts like a bitch, I'm just glad you guys didn't kill me," I snap back, and I see her face fall slightly like she felt guilty. Damn good job making me feel like an asshole.

She closes her eyes and takes a deep, calming breath and then sits in the chair that the doc was sitting in. "I'm sorry about that. That is definitely not how we do things here, and trust me, Sabrina, has to deal with her consequences," she reassures.

"Good, at least I know you guys aren't usually murderers, but can we please get this interview done? I would like to be locked up with my partner now so I know if she's okay," I try to push.

"You really don't care that you're about to be locked up? Why?" she asks Oh. My. God, She is either new at leading or this is her strategy; all I know is I'm not looking for new friends. I'm trying to keep the few I have left safe, and she is preventing that.

I lean in. "Listen, all I care about is not dying, making sure I'm healthy, my partner is okay, and you let me go eventually. If that means sucking it up and playing by your rules for a little while, I will, but don't expect me to be happy, or expect me to want to be here long. I don't care if I need to be locked away for a little while if that's what it takes. I don't follow anyone, so if you want me to stay and be your servant..." I trail off and laugh sarcastically. "Then your friend Sabrina should have shot me through the head," I finish. She looks taken aback for a second. "What? Left you speechless? Yeahhh, I have that effect on people," I say, and the corner of my mouth curls up to a sly smirk.

She shifts in her seat and clears her throat. "No.. it's just, I like your attitude. If you finish answering the questions and you and your friend be on ya'll's best behavior for a little while, I'm sure me and the others will have no problem letting you guys go. Ryder probably wants to kick you guys out now," she jokes slightly. "Anyway, you said the rest of your people died from the lack of supplies, but when we caught you guys, you guys had bags of supplies. How?" she asks, but before I go to speak, she raises her hand and cuts me off. "Keep in mind we interviewed your friend already and we know some things already. I like you and all, but these are MY people, and I'll do what I have to so that I can keep them safe," she says confidently; that's the most leader-like I've seen her.

Based off what they told me it sounds like Miko resisted the details, so they're looking for me to do the same. They want details, they want to know something about us, I'll give them that. Well, a fabricated, dramatic and vague version of the details. I look at her. "Well, you know my name, uhh, I'm nineteen, I lost everything and all that generic story. Yes, there were a few of us before. I was in charge of the group. Some left, and some joined along the way if we allowed them too. Recently, we started dealing with hard times; it was like one thing after another." I feel my body start to tense, my breath starts to get stuck in my throat, and my hands start to shake. I try to calm myself down, but the memories completely break through their little tucked away door and start flooding my head, and I look down to the floor. The pain in my shoulder is easing up thankfully; the medication is kicking in. "I-I couldn't save them, I tried, we all tried. Eventually, we started to run low on supplies, but we had a tough scenario. I couldn't go out because I was recovering from an injury. Miko was dealing with the loss of one of our friends, and the others in the group were either too weak or inexperienced to go out. We needed to wait. The day Miko and I left our friends, or friends tried to follow…" I trail off. "Before I finish, I want to know more about everything," I tell her.

"You know my name is Claire, and you know there are four of us who run everything. We aren't actually that different than you and your friend's old group; we are all mid-teen and early twenty- year-olds with no adults. I'm twenty-one. There are a total of sixteen of us. Most live in that abandoned building. This is the closest thing to our medical/supply building, and the house is where the four of us leaders live." She gives me a rough breakdown of the area, but I still have no idea how far I am from my people. I need to ask, but she can't know where they are… "Where were you guys coming from, when you got to that house?" she asks; does she know about the house already?

"We were coming from the woods, we kinda just been stumbling along these past—"

"No, no, where are the rest of your dead people?" she asks and leans in with an eyebrow raised. "If you had a group, you had to have shelter, because a group of more than three can't make it without at least somewhere," she states.

"You have no idea what it was like. Nor do you have the right to tell me how my people were able to survive. You wanna know how we survived for a while? We had a minivan for a loooooong time, and once that was gone, we didn't have nowhere to go, at all." I keep a cold-stoned face while telling the obvious lie. "If you don't believe me, or whatever it is, I really don't care, we stumbled onto that house. The supplies? I'll show you personally where we got them if that's what you really want. Now, I'm done with your questions," I tell her. I know that being this bold is really a dangerous move, but something tells me this girl isn't as tough as she thinks she is.

"You know, you have a really bold mouth. That could get you into a lot of trouble here," she threatens.

"I like trouble, it gives this meaningless life a little bit more action and meaning." I shrug her off. She is getting on my nerves now. We are done with this whole interview, and I barely learned anything.

"You know what? I think we are done today. Come on. I'll show you where your friend is and where you will be staying." She stands up and motions to the door.

I stand up and feel my pockets; of course they took everything. I look around the room and don't even see my bag. "Uh, where is my stuff?" I ask.

"The bag is with your friend. It's empty, obviously, and our weapons are away. At least we let you keep your personal belongings," she tries to reason.

"Yes, because keeping my bag makes up for shooting me, and stealing my stuff," I snap slightly. I can see her eyes look sad but then turn dark and cold.

"Anything to protect my family," is all she says before leaving and me following behind her. Outside, I see a few mini fires spread out, chairs, and coolers. It looks like a set up for a family having a barbeque. She takes me to a cellar, which is right behind this little hospital house. "This is where your friend is, and where you will be staying. Someone will be back tomorrow morning to get you guys. Do everyone a favor, when you talk to Ryder alone, play nice." She opens it and points downstairs.

I roll my eyes and walk downstairs without looking back. I hear the doors close behind me and see Miko sitting against the wall sleeping. She had a busted lip. Guess the Q&A really didn't go over nicely. "Miko!" I whisper and kick her slightly, and she stirs awake.

Her eyes blink open slowly, but when she sees it's me she jumps up. "Finally! I thought they killed your ass for being a smartass." She half laughs with a very poorly covered sigh of relief from worrying.

"I thought the same, guess it did go bad." I point to her lip. She looks at me, confused, as if her lip isn't busted.

"Ohhh." She touches her lip and laughs uncomfortably. "Yeah, you're not gonna believe what happened. When they took you into the building, I wanted to go in, but they kept saying no and pulling me away. They took me to a room right next to yours and started asking me questions, and I didn't want to answer because they wouldn't let me see you. I'm not gonna lie, I may have started it. I hit the girl who was standing next to me and...Daniel hit me..." She trails off. "Can you believe it!? That dude is alive! And in charge of a new group already!" She scoffs. She takes a few seconds, sighs out, and sits down. "I've been here for hours, worried that..." She stops.

"Worried about that..." I try to press on.

"That I was stuck here, and that you were gone!" she snaps, then takes a deep breath. "I'm sorry, I just don't want anyone else dying because of me," she says.

"Woah, no one's death is on your hands. You never killed unless you had to, and you did everything you could to protect everyone," I try to reassure her, but she instead brushes me off.

"You...you don't know that, Miranda. There is still a lot about me you don't know, believe it or not." She nervously chuckles. "You have no idea how I feel. I know I could have done more. First, I didn't think I'd care, but I guess after twenty-four hours a day there is nothing left for me to do but to think, and the more I think about it the more I regret so many actions I can't even count." She finally seems to breathe out everything that she's probably been holding in since Kev died.

"I know what I'm about to say is gonna sound cliche, but you can't change the past, Miko. Life is forever moving on; the past has to be nothing but what it is because we can't dwell on the past and we can't stress over the future either. All we can do is..." I pause for a sec and take a look around the cellar. "Try to sleep in whatever this is. And tomorrow we figure out how to leave," I finish.

She doesn't say anything for a minute. I try to speak again but she hold her hand up "Thank you, for everything, Miranda. Seriously. I don't say it often and I mean it." She hugs me.

We say goodnight. There are two dirty, beat-up air mattresses with sheets and a pillow each. The others won't be worrying about us until at least dusk, so that means we have at least one full day in this place. There has to be something up with Daniel. I'm gonna try and talk to him and figure how the hell he ended up here. Oh, and for the busted lip he gave Miko. I will kick Ryder's ass tomorrow if he tries anything, and I really hope no one tries talking to me. I'm not in the mood for new friends. This is gonna be an interesting day.

*   *   *

The next morning, Ryder and Daniel came down banging their pistols on everything that was metal or would make noise. "Rise and shine lovelies," Ryder says, laughing and jumping up and down.

We both jump and sit up from bed. "We are up, assholes! Can you please stop yelling and banging things?" I groan and yawn.

They stop, and Ryder pats Daniel on the back. "Tell them what to do. I got better shit to do," he says smugly and runs out.

Once the cellar doors slam shut, I kick Daniel from in my bed. "Ow" he winches. "I guess I deserved that, but seriously, guys, we don't have much time. Miranda, you're with Claire and Ryder's group today. Miko, you're with Destiny and me. Anyway, I'm trying to get you guys out of here, but you have to let me know if my brother is okay first," he explains.

"Jake's fine, but he won't be fine for longer, the longer we are stuck in here," Miko says; she's already standing by now and looks like she's definitely ready to hit him.

I stand up too. "How are you trying to get us out of here, exactly?" I ask.

"Every two days I'm supposed to go out alone at dawn and scoop out the land for anything new at one of its most sensitive hours in my opinion." That second day is tomorrow. The group knows about it, we were gonna make it a whole man thing, but I figured it's better alone. No one is up at that time, so it will be the perfect time for you guys to leave with me," he finishes explaining.

Miko looks Daniel up and down for a very long time. "You do anything to fuck us over and I promise your brother is as good as dead," she finally says.

"Miko!" I shout, stunned. How she could just… I don't know

Daniel simply waves me off. "I deserve it. Miranda, go upstairs. Claire is upstairs with Ryder, probably waiting for you," he tells me.

I step to Daniel. He is only a few inches taller than me, so I don't end up look up and make him look like he's intimidating, 'cause he really isn't. "Anything happens to me or her with these people out there today, I'm holding you responsible, Daniel. Don't screw it up." I push past him on my way out. Claire was the only one waiting for me when I got up from the cellar "Where's sharky?" I joke. She chuckles slightly.

"You guys would be an awesome duo if you two weren't so alike, but come on, he's in the complex with the other two that are joining us," she starts walking and motions for me to follow.

"Never say we are alike again," I tell her.

She laughs. "Ohh yeah?" she says. "You're in my playground now, I'll say whatever I want," she says jokingly; feels like she isn't trying to make me feel like what I so obviously am, a prisoner.

"Okay then." I shrug her off; neither of us say anything for the next very awkward two more minutes of walking. Maybe I did seem like an asshole. I just don't want to make friends.

As soon as we enter the building I feel a sharp stinging pain in my shoulder; my hand immediately goes to where the bullet hit, and I stop in my tracks to focus on trying not to let the pain get over me. I lean on the wall. "Hey, are you okay?" Claire asks. I feel warm liquid slowly seeping through my shirt. "Fuck, your wound opened again." She points.

I shake my head. "No shit. My shoulder… Fuck ,the next day, why does it always hurt more?" I groan in pain.

Claire takes my other arm. "Come on, Julia's door is the second door on the right here. When we get there, I got medicine and bandages in my pocket," she tells me. She helps me into the girl's room. "Ryder, get up, Miranda needs to sit in the chair." Ryder just snickers and crosses his legs.

"She can sit on the bed, I don't mind," a soft voice to my left says. I turn to see a young light-skinned girl, hazel eyes, and jet-black hair. She couldn't be more than fifteen years old. I take a second, then look between Julia and Ryder; they're siblings.

"Thank you," I say, and Claire helps me sit. She touches my shirt. "Damn, you bled through your shirt. But if you want your bandages changed, you need to take your shirt off. Here, take these." She hands me two pain pills and takes out bandages and peroxide.

"I'm good, it's fine," I try to reassure. I really just don't want to disinfect it. "Bullshit, you need to clean and rebandage it so it doesn't get infected. If you want Ryder and Julia to step out, then, guys, get out for a sec. Close the door and wait for Frank; if he shows up tell him we will be out in a sec to go," she tells Ryder. The two of them leave, and Claire snaps her attention back to me. "Off," she snaps.

"Why the hell do you even care!? You're just wasting your supplies on a prisoner." I try to stand up but she straight-arm pushes me back down.

"Just because we took you guys doesn't mean you are our prisoners," she says. I laugh. "If anything I don't understand why you're being a hard-ass! You guys have been by yourselves for a very long time now. You should be glad we took ya! Just listen to what you're told for once. We want you guys to adjust. Damn it, Miranda, though, you're making it hard for Daniel and me to keep arguing for you guys to stay!" she snaps. "You know what, don't clean it. I don't care, but the second you get too sick…" She leans in. "Don't look for me for saving when they want to kill you." Definitely know why she is one of the leaders now. I'm actually intimidated a little.

She throws the bandages and peroxide at me and heads towards the door. "Wait," I sigh out. "I need help, I can't clean it by myself," I ask. She stops in her tracks but doesn't look back.

"I offered my help, I tried to be nice, I tried to be as welcoming as possible given the current situation. Yet, you were still an asshole. Why should I help you now?" she asks.

"Because I'm sorry for my actions. I'm not use to others wanting to take care of me. The only other person I had that use to do stuff like clean my wounds, they aren't here anymore. And I hate peroxide," I half-lie. She turns around without another word and grabs the stuff she threw and stands there. "Why are yo— Ohh." I take off my shirt and the old bandages. "You're not into girls, right? I don't gotta worry about you, right?" I try to joke., She cracks a smile and firmly shakes her head no.

"Nope, so don't flatter yourself." She laughs quietly. She goes to dab a cloth of peroxide on my shoulder, but my hand shoots up and grabs her wrist. "Uhh, gotta let me clean it." She tries to shake free.

I put my head down and quickly whisper out a mumbled, "I'm scared." She leans in as if she didn't hear me and I look up. "I said…I'm scared. I don't like cleaning wounds, never have," I admit.

She shakes her head with an amusing smile plastered to her face. "It's nice to know you're not a total hard-ass, but seriously, you gotta let go. You can hold my hand," she jokes but hands me the hand I'm now holding captive. I take her hand hesitantly and let go of the other one "One…two…

three," she counts down and carefully dabs the cloth on the opened hole in my shoulder. I squeeze her hand and tense until she stops dabbing it. "I just need to wrap it up again and you're done. See, wasn't that bad," she says.

I relax, let go of her hand, and drop my shoulders. "No, let's just get it over with." I try to rush. "What exactly are we doing today?" I ask.

"We have the joy of going into the city that isn't but two miles east of these woods by car. We need to go and see if there are any supplies. The winter is coming, and I'm not sure if we have enough supplies when things get too cold to hunt. Especially with two new people," she explains; her words are definitely backed with panic.

"You guys have a car?" I ask.

"Yeah, Frank's dad was a mechanic, so he saw he knows a few things, and he found this truck full of gas that only needed a new motor, and I think the taillight was busted. He spent forever looking for the parts he needed, but he got it working again, so let's just hope it isn't too dangerous," she finishes explaining.

"God, I haven't seen anything resembling a city since all this started." I laughed in disbelief. I've always seen how the world looked in all these zombie movies, games, etc. Let me tell you, they got most of it spot on, expect for the fact that the developer's writers all of a sudden think the sun and light from the world is drained and there is never any color anywhere anymore.

We leave the room, and everyone is waiting right by the door. "Hey, you must be the newbie, I'm Frank." This scrappy young guy holds out his hand, and I shake it firmly. "Hey, nice grip," he comments as he pulls his hand away. I roll my eyes. "So, ready to go?" He jingles the keys.

Ryder snatches the keys from Frank's hands. "Yeah, and I'm driving." Before anyone could rebuttal, he walks out.

Frank's face drops and he hangs his head low as he drags his feet and follows after Ryder; it's like if Ryder just killed a puppy right in front of him. "Not to come off harshly to you two, but I really don't wanna go anywhere with that guy. And if you really want me to be useful and not cause problems…" I trail off and shrug.

"Let's just go," Claire says. I hope Miko is having a better time with Daniel.

MIKO'S POV

Will Miranda be mad if I killed Daniel too? I think if he comes back still breathing she can't get mad. Right now we are in their storage/supply room taking inventory. Daniel and Destiny are an item; they have not stopped flirting and kissing since we picked her up. I swear to God I feel like I should leave them alone in this damn closet. "Can either of you tell me why we are counting cans of beans and bullets?" I groan, annoyed. I lost track already like, three times which cans I've counted for or not 'cause every time I try to focus, I hear... *"Babe! Come help me."* Destiny's super high-pitch, girly voice right behind me and Daniel coming to her saying, *"Oh, well, of course,"* then a ton of giggling, and for some reason they think this is a master bedroom and pushes and brushes around me. I swear it's like I'm babysitting children who just found out there was another gender.

"We count supplies to make sure things don't go missing," Destiny snaps. Oh bitch... I am not the one. I turn to her, stunned.

Daniel puts a calming hand on Destiny, clearly seeing me tense up. "We do it for our safety. The first months here, Destiny said they were robbed, so now people come in everyday, count, and keep track," Daniel explains.

"Thank you, Daniel." I force a fake smile and turn back and pick up a can to start counting again.

I'm assuming everything is okay because I hear Daniel mumbling shit to her until I hear her say, "Is there a problem that bitch has with me?" to Daniel.

This time the can I had in my hand I smashed on the grown, it busted, beans and all the liquid splatters all over the floor, my shoes and wall next to me "who are you calling a bitch" I turn around and this time I step face to face with her "if you have anything you wanna say to me, you say it to me. Not your bitch-ass boyfriend," I snap harshly. She just laughs.

"I said you're a bitch. And, aww, are you mad? You want my boyfriend?" she teases. Is she serious?

"No, but your little boyfriend wants my friend; as a matter of fact, she had him first." I smirk. Her eyes go wide and she looks between Daniel and me.

"Is she telling the truth? But...but how?" she stutters out. Daniel doesn't say anything; instead, he glares at me. "ANSWER ME!" Destiny yells. This girl is psycho.

"I-I uhh," he stutters.

"Told you," I point out smugly. Next thing I feel is a sting across my cheek and my head jerks to the left. THIS BITCH SLAPPED ME! My hand shoots up to my cheek and I take a sec to gather my thoughts. She looks at me with a big, satisfied grin, but her eyes are still shooting daggers. The next and last thing I remember is grabbing Destiny by her shirt and slamming her against the shelfs. I hear her back slam against the metal bar of the shelf, seeing her slide down and Daniel picking me up and throwing me outside the closet.

…Well that could have, haha…you know…

I decide it's probably not the best idea to go back in there, so I walk outside to get some fresh air. I don't know what's gotten into me lately, but I really don't like it. It's all Robert's fault! Daniel, he was there and didn't do shit. Fuck them. I need to relax. I see this little girl drawing and sitting down on a beach chair. She doesn't look to be older than fourteen. I walk up to try and get a better look at the drawing; it's a beach sunset…. Wow, she's really talented. "Um, can I help you?" a soft voice breaks my trance.

"Oh shi— shoot. I'm sorry, I didn't mean to stare. My little cousin used to draw all the time; she was just as talented as you." I feel a soft smile on my lips.

The girl smiles widely. "Thank you, My name is Rachel, what's yours?" she asks.

"Miko, and if you don't mind me asking, how old are you?" I ask. I know I'm being nosy, but I rather be doing this then back there.

"I…I think my birthday just passed right around this week or so, so fifteen" she says. I was close.

"I'm around eighteen," I guess. I know Miranda's birthday should be around this month too. The days are shorter, so fall is coming, so maybe we can celebrate when we get back. I see her smile immediately drop when I say how old I am. I want to ask why, but before I can, I see a pick-up truck pull up right next to us and see Miranda, Claire, and some guy in the back.

"What are you doing here? I thought I told Daniel that he had you today?" Claire asks.

"I uh, well, you see, uhh…" I try to explain but the words don't seem to come out. I look for Miranda in panic, and she taps Claire and whispers something in her ear.

"You're lucky I always pack spare weapons. Get in," Claire says and scoots so I can sit in between her and Miranda.

"Thank you," I whisper to Miranda.

"Of course. Anytime, troublemaker," she whispers and shoves me slightly.

MIRANDA'S POV

It's kind of ironic that Miko is the one getting in trouble and I'm not but go figure. The moment she looks at me I know something had happened that was definitely her fault, and I'm probably gonna end up arguing with her later about it. But I knew she needed help. I told Claire that Miko is better at supply runs and is an excellent shot, and she trusted me enough to let her get in. It's kind of sad, I don't know, I don't wanna stay but…maybe the others can come back with us? Or they can come with us? We need to talk about it for sure. The ride was definitely tense and bumpy; no one spoke, and I'm guessing it's because Miko joined without an explanation. When we exit the woods into the highway, I can't help but look at every single detail of the dotted-lined road covered in blood, guts, bullet casings, broken parts of every car, and weapons and dead bodies, some just little kids. I see this horrific sight and all I can seem to think about is how I haven't seen a street in forever and how much I missed driving in cars. It's like this stuff doesn't even phase me anymore; should I be happy about that? 'Cause I am. The cars are all flipped over, ransacked through and destroyed; the smell of death somehow reeked worse than inside the woods, and I can't help but gag slightly, and Claire chuckles. "The smell in the city is definitely stronger. More people lived there, but don't worry, I got weapons and bandanas for everyone." She reaches inside her bag and pulls out three guns, and gives one to both Miko and I, then pulls out four bandanas. One blue, purple, red, and yellow. "Which one do you want? I call purple," she offers. Miko instantly grabs red, and I take blue, leaving Julia with the yellow. "Now I'm not even gonna sugarcoat it, the smell is going to be really bad the more city we enter. There are a lot more dead survivors and rotten," she warns. "Please don't puke."

The rest of the ride was filled with us covering our noses and mouths. The car suddenly stopped short of a really dirty, run-down and broken gas station. The store's windows were all busted, gasoline leaked out all around the gas pumps, blood splatter everywhere, and looking inside, half of the shelves are turned over, some very unlucky workers dead all over. "Yeahh, no offense but this looks like a total bust," Miko states, and I stifle back my laugh.

"Not only that it reeks of gasoline and death, this shit could blow at any moment," I say, while Ryder and Frank hopping out the truck with gas masks.

"Aww are the babies sick about the smell? Grow up." Ryder snickers.

Claire is the first to jump out and slaps Ryder upside the head. "Stop," Claire demands. "Miko, me, and Julia are going inside while Miranda, Ryder, and Frank stay around here, check out the corpse, and see what you can find." I cringe; first, taking orders is totally new to me, but two, why does she insist on leaving me with this man?

Claire and the other two walk into the store, and Ryder immediately starts walking to the gas pumps alone. "Where are you going?" Frank shouts.

"To go do as I'm told, duh." Ryder just shrugs.

I scoff, and Frank just places his hand on my shoulder. "You can stay by the car if you want; watch the back of the store and what's coming," Frank tries to suggest. I take a deep breath, then brush him off.

"I think I'll just take the back of the store." I walk away. As I'm walking passed the store I hear loud bangs coming from within. "That's really loud, hope it's not too loud," I whisper. When I reach the back of the store, I freeze in my steps. I see at least dozens of zombies coming from a little while in. I run back to the guys. "Frank, Ryder!" I yell, and they both turn, and I guess they saw what I saw 'cause I see Frank's jaw drop.

"Fuck what are we gonna do?" Frank asks.

"We gotta go tell the others it's time to go" I say.

"No, we need them to get those supplies, we gotta take care of them" he doesn't even look at us, his eyes locked on the swarm. "Check, make sure your guns are loaded" he tells us, when neither Frank or I move, he grabs our guns and quickly examines the chambers and pulls out two more full ones and three suppressors from his back pockets giving all of us two rounds of ammo and gives us secrecy.

"This is crazy, man. We need to tell them," Frank tries to reason, but Ryder just shakes his head.

"I know we are all good shots, just stay a good distance away. Plus, they won't hear it. Come on." Before Frank or I can try say something again, Ryder sprints to the back.

"Good luck," Frank says, with doubt and fear written all over his face.

"Good luck, we got this," I try to reassure, and we sprint after Ryder.

MIKO'S POV

I'm so glad I didn't get stuck with Ryder, but I do kinda feel bad for Miranda 'cause I know she doesn't get along with him either. Claire snaps her finger in front of my face. "Hey, I need you to try and pick the lock of the pharmacy." She points.

"And you think I know how to pick a lock because…?" I ask.

"Uhhh, 'cause I'm taking a guess." She shrugs; since when do I look like a lockpicker?

"Sure, I'll give it a go." I take a quick look and find a hammer covered in blood. "This should work; break the damn door open." I laugh.

"Do you think that's gonna work?" Julia asks.

"No idea, but I'm gonna find out," I say. Thankfully, all I should have to do is knock the knob off and we should be good. I place the hammer on top of the knob. "This might be a little loud," I warn as I raise my arm and bring the hammer down as hard as I can. Nothing, again this time the knob bends. The others definitely hear the loud banging. Hopefully it's just them. After eight good times, the knob finally falls and I drop the hammer; the tension in my arm and hand ache, but at least it's open. "So who's going first? Because I'm not." Nope, that's how you die in horror movies.

Claire holds her gun to the door and kicks it open. She takes a quick look inside. "There is a zombie in here but they're pinned under a desk. If we just keep away we should be good." She motions for us to follow. There were a ton of medical supplies, from pills to needles, bandages, enough to keep a group of their size alive a lot longer than they should be. "Come on, gather as much as these bags fill." She hands us little bookbags and starts packing. We pick the place clean; our bookbags all filled to the max. "Let's go," Claire says. We make it outside, and Ryder, Frank, and Miranda are nowhere to we found. "Guys!" Claire whispers/yells. "We don't have time for this!" Claire looks around the front; the truck is still here, so they didn't leave, and if they did, they haven't gotten far.

Suddenly, we hear someone yell, "Over here!"

Claire quickly drops her bookbag. "Give Julia your bag, and Julia, you take the bags to the truck, and you don't move from the back; you're with me," Claire says handing her bag and my bag to Julia. We reach the back of the store and see Ryder, Miranda, and Frank surrounded by zombies. "What the hell happened?" Claire asks, concerned.

"Nothing, it's taken care of," Ryder says.

"Uh, not nothing." Claire tries to push on, pointing to the corpses behind us.

"Well, it's done with now, so can we please—" In the middle of Ryder snapping we hear Julia scream, and before anyone could blink, Ryder runs to the truck. There are zombies around the truck, and you can see Julia trying to hit them away. "Get away from her!" Ryder yells, shooting them all. "Julia! Julia! Are you okay?" He jumps in the back holding his crying baby sister tightly to his chest. One of them managed to grab her bandanna. I picked the once yellow bandana up from the now really dead hand of the zombie and it was covered in dirt and what looked like blood, making the bandana almost seem orange when held to the light. Out of the corner of my eye I can see Claire staring at the bandana too, thinking what I'm thinking. No one really knows what to do or say right now; all we hear is the shushing of Ryder and the soft, muffled whimpers of his sister through his shirt. I tuck the bandana in my back pocket and jump in the back.

"Let's go. We need to make sure she's okay," Claire says. "Frank, you drive, I'll be up front with you. You two, get in." She just points and heads to the front.

…. This is gonna be one long way back….

MIRANDA'S POV

I saw when Miko held up Julia's bandana, there was blood on it…. I know we are all hoping that it was one of the zombie's blood, but it looks too bright to be. We all know this, no one wants to say it though. *When you say it out loud, it's real.* The only thing I can focus on right now is the truckbed floor. I really hope the others are okay. I really need to find out what happened with Miko and Daniel before this, but now with Julia being like this, I doubt I'll get answers. Fuck that, I need my answers now. My thoughts are interrupted when I hear Julia coughing; not a little cold cough, it was hard, dry, almost as if it was forced. My head jerks up at just the right time to see her cough up blood all over Ryder's shirt "I…I'm sorry." Julia breathes out; her eyes are bloodshot, and she's dripping in sweat.

"It's okay, sis. Just stay strong, we are almost back," Ryder's voice cracks at the end. For the first time this guy really seems broken and scared.

We make it back to camp and Ryder jumps out with his sister in his arms right into their "hospital." Claire and Frank jump out too. Claire stops and turns to Miko and I. "This…this doesn't look good for Julia. Please, just stay out of everyone's way," she begs before taking off after the others.

"Reminds you of your brother?" Miko asks.

I nod slightly. "Reminds you of your sister?" I shoot back, and she nods back. "What happened, before we left?" I ask, I see her tense and sigh out heavily.

"Destiny and I got into a fight because Daniel and her are a thing and she thought I was jealous of them. So…" Miko trails off and swallows hard.

"Finish."

"I might have snapped and confessed that we knew Daniel before this and hit Destiny. I don't think Daniel is gonna help us now," she finishes.

"Are you serious? Miko!" I groan and put my face into my hands.

"I know, I screwed up. I'm so sorry," she says. I can hear in her voice that she is actually sorry about this. *But it doesn't help that now we are stuck here.* "I know it doesn't," I hear her mumble. Opps, must have said that out loud.

Frank comes out of the hospital. "How is she?" I ask, and Frank shakes his head.

"She got bit, right in her side. We are going to take her now somewhere to…you know…" he trails and coughs. "Anyway, you guys got a room in the building and I'm here to show you." He motions for us to follow him into the building. We were on the first floor in a small studio apartment. "Just stay here," is all he says before closing the door.

ALLISON'S POV

"Alex! Look!" I point through the bushes to a car pulling up to the old house that Miranda and Miko should have been in. "Stay here with Jake. I'm going to go see what it is," I whisper and try to walk through the bushes, but Alex grabs my arm to stop me.

"We all go together. I rather us all take on, God knows how many people are in there, than just you" Alex warns. I nod because I know he makes sense. We sneak our way over to another bush a little closer to the now parked car. The passenger seat door bursts open, and a guy jumps out first, then I see two girls, one older, one younger, sit up from the back of the truck. The younger girl looks really sick. Alex and I take a quick look at each other…. We both know what's wrong.

I see another guy jump out from the passenger side of the truck. I guess he was in the back. He jumps out and turns around. "Daniel," I whisper. I see Jake gasp and try to make a break for it. I quickly grab him and cover his mouth so I know he won't yell. "Shh, we have to be quiet. We have to make sure Daniel is okay," I tell Jake quietly, and he just looks away.

"Give me her," I hear the guy say as he picks up the younger girl. Now that I have a better look, the little girl's shirt is covered in blood and teared; she is gasping ever-so-slightly for breath. The driver door now opens, and another guy jumps out, shorter and scrawnier than the other one.

"We gotta take her downstairs," Daniel says, motioning to the house. They all run in.

"This just got a whole lot harder," Alex whispers. "We just wanted to find the girls, but this…we stumbled onto some real issues," he warns.

I sigh. I know he is right, but there isn't much we can do anymore. "Look, it's either we keep going and find our friends or give up. You can do whatever. I'm finding Miranda and Miko," I break it down to him. He rolls his eyes but doesn't move. I know he is with me. We quietly walk up to the truck and peek inside the bed of the truck, and it's soaked in blood. "That little girl doesn't have much time left," I whisper/yell to Alex who is inspecting the driver's side, Jack clinging to his leg.

"Should we just take the car? We just drive the direction they're coming from. I'm sure we will find somewhere," Alex suggests; he peeks his head in. "The keys aren't in the ignition, but they're on the dash." He reaches his hand in to grab the keys, but the keys are just out of reach. "Damn it," he groans and keeps trying.

"I'm going to go check what's going on downstairs," I whisper to Alex. "Stay with Alex; don't follow me," I tell Jake and quietly inch my way inside the house slowly.

The house is really quiet. Every step I take I can hear the creek on the floor. I reach the top of the staircase and I can hear muffled voices arguing. *"Over my dead body!"* That definitely isn't Daniel's voice; it's probably the older and scarier-looking guy's voice. I tip-toe downstairs and put my ear to the door. "She is already dying! Once she's dead we won't have much time, Ryder," I hear Daniel say.

"No one is laying a fucking hand on my sister!" I'm assuming Ryder screams.

I turn to leave and nearly jump out of my skin to see Jake standing behind me. "What are you doing?" I whisper. He just points to the door, and I sigh. "Not now, Jake." I try to motion him to go upstairs, and he shakes his head. We hear a scream, and without thinking, I bust open the door just in time to see what the screaming was about.

The little girl had turned. "Allison! Jake!" Daniel freezes when he sees the two of us.

"Daniel, look out!" Ryder pushes Daniel out of the way of the little girl coming right at him and tries holding the girl back from biting him.

"Kill that thing!" the other guy yells. Ryder trips back and falls, with the little girl falling on top of him. Next thing I know, the older girl pulls out her gun and blows the little girl's brains out. The guy Ryder jumps up and tackles the girl with the gun. "Ryder! Get off!" The guy I still yet to know his name yells. Daniel and he pull Ryder off the girl, and Ryder takes off out the basement. *Shit Alex, gotta hurry.*

"Who the fuck are these people, Daniel, and how the fuck do you know them?" the girl says, pointing her gun directly at me. I put my hands up.

"Look, we—" I try to say, but Daniel cuts me off

"He's my brother…she's an old friend," Daniel caves. She looks at him in disbelief for a second. She takes a closer look between Jake and Daniel and slowly lowers her gun.

"I'm Claire, he's Frank." She points to the guy just standing there watching. "And the other one was Ryder. Your names?" she asks.

"Allison. The little one is Jake. Who was she?" I point to the dead little girl not even five feet from us.

Claire's eyes slowly followed my finger's direction, seeing the girl's body. She gasped slightly and quickly turned her head, closing her eyes tight. She takes in a shaky deep breath and blinks back a few tears before looking up at me again. "Julia, Ryder's sister," she chokes out before turning her head again; this time I see a teardrop roll down her cheek and hit the floor.

"Where's Miko and Miranda?" I ask, looking directly at Daniel.

Claire's head snaps up. "You know, Miranda… and Miko too." She trails off. She scoffs and shakes her head. "Of course, I know they were too comfortable to be all alone. And Miranda doesn't seem like the lonely duo type. How?" is all she asks.

"I would love to explain this to you right now, but Alex is up there with your friend—" Daniel cuts me off… Oh, I get how Miranda feels now.

"Shit." He runs upstairs. We all follow behind. When we get outside, Alex and Ryder are surrounded by zombies slashing and shooting. "Where the hell did they all come from!" Daniel yells.

I point to the back of the house near the wooded area where I see the dusty, dirty fog they pick up when they walk in huge herds. "Everyone, back to the truck!" Claire says through popping bullets. Frank, Daniel, and Jake all jump into the front. Clarie, Alex, and I jump down into the truck-bed and we speed off in the opposite direction.

"Holy shit, that was close." Alex breathes out, panting. I swallow hard and just nod in agreement. "When we get back to wherever the hell you guys are taking us, we want our friends, then we will be on our way," Alex immediately switches the tone and tells Claire. She doesn't say a word, instead just turns her head to the side to look at the road.

…This isn't going to be easy…

RYDER'S POV

When my sister's body dropped mine dropped with her. She was all I had left… the only reason I had for being here, and I failed her. I should have fucking been there. Everyone hates me; my only purpose in life is standing behind a gun barrel. 'Cause God knows I couldn't even be a good big brother. Seeing Frank keep side-eyeing me only made my blood boil more. "I'm fine," is all I could blurt out. He stopped looking at me after that. *Fuck me, my arm hurts.* I wince and look down. What I saw made my heart stop and drop straight to my ass. I quickly pull down my sleeve and fold my arms.

… I can't go down like this…

MIRANDA'S POV

They are taking forever. Everyone knows they should have been back by now. First time I saw everybody outside, Miko and I are sitting right outside the building. Some of the armed guys are with Destiny pacing, some people are smoking off by the house. Guess everyone's on edge.

"They should have been back by now," Miko states. I nod and click my teeth.

"Something is wrong, and I feel it," I whisper to her.

Not too long after the car's engine can be heard and I can make out two other people in the back other than Claire's. The car finally pulls up and holy shit… "Allison! Alex!" Miko gasps and hesitates to jump and run to two of them.

Frank and Ryder hop out of the truck first. Ryder motions for Destiny and the other guards to come closer, and he draws his gun on Miko and I, while the others draw theirs on Alex, Allison, Jake, and Daniel. "Now…I think a couple of people got some explaining to do," Ryder says with a cocky smirk. "You four, join your friends and kneel in front of me, with your hands where we can see them." He points aimlessly behind him to the others. The six of us take a knee and have our hands behind our heads. I see the few other teens watching in horror and fear behind Ryder and his group.

"What do you want?" I ask, and Ryder laughs.

"It's pretty obvious what we all want. An explanation. Then if it's good enough we see how it goes on letting you guys live," Ryder says. Out of the corner of my eye, I see Claire, and her hand is twitching right about her gun holster as she shoots daggers into the back of Ryder's head. Here's my chance; we didn't work this hard for a couple of wanna-be thugs to take us out now.

"This can't be how you want to run things, Claire!" I plead with her, and she looks at me, her face softening seeing all of us shaking and Jake quietly sobbing. "Please, I know Daniel kept us from you guys, but I promise if you let us explain, without GUNS to our heads, you will get your answers. Come on, don't you get any say in this!" I beg, and Claire shakes her head.

"Destiny is all for whatever Ryder wants to do with you guys. I…I'm out numbered here." She shrugs, helpless.

Ryder lets off a warning shot in front of me. "I'm getting impatient. Next shot won't miss," he threatens.

Daniel speaks up. "My brother and I were with Miranda's group for a little while. We had got caught up with a bad guy…who hurt us, and we wanted help. Miranda and her friends gave it to us." Daniel breaks to look at me with a sad smile before looking back up at Ryder. "And I was stupid after receiving their help to run. I got scared of finally being on my own. Miranda kept my brother so he would be safe, and I didn't tell you guys I guess because I wanted to forget… I wanted to start a new life," Daniel explains.

Ryder doesn't respond at first. He just stares, his eyes turning bloodshot. "You all lied to us. How can we ever trust any of you again!" Ryder yells his hands pale, the gun trembling.

"Ryder, please. Let's just let them go. If they come back they know the consequences," Claire tries to plead. Ryder just shakes his head and starts hacking. "Uhh, are you okay?" Claire asks Ryder.

Ryder spits out blood. His eyes widen and he wipes his lip. "Yeah… just must be getting sick." Before Claire can protest, Ryder starts coughing and spitting up blood again.

"He's more than sick," I say, and everyone looks at me confused. "I know that cough, I know those eyes… I know what spitting up blood means, Ryder. You know it too; you want to tell everyone or should I—" Before I can react, Ryder hits me with the barrel of the gun on the right side of my face to shut me up and knocking me to the ground.

"Ryder!" Claire, Daniel, and Destiny all yell at the same time. Claire drops to her knees and inspects my face, which now has a huge cut and bruise forming along my jaw.

"Shut up!" Ryder pushes Claire to the floor, yanking me to my feet, and brings the gun to my forehead. "One good reason not to blow your sorry brains out right now. We all know I ain't got shit left to live for anyway," Ryder says, laughing psychotically.

"Do you really want your last moment here before turning to be killing someone in cold blood? Is that what Julia would have wanted?" I ask. Ryder's eyes narrow.

"What is she talking about, Ry?" Destiny hesitantly asks as she slowly walks up to Ryder. Ryder holds his hand up for her to stop, and drops his head in defeat. He nods his head towards everyone as if he just allowed me to tell everyone.

"He's been bitten," is all I say. Ryder puts his gun in his holster and yanks his sleeve up. Everyone gasps seeing the purplish red veins bulging from his forearm up to his elbow and further. You can clearly see the teeth marks and where the infection started to sprout from. "It was Julia…wasn't it?" I ask. Ryder nods slowly.

"Damn it, Ry," Destiny huffs, combing her hands through her hair nervously. "What are we going to do?" she asks.

"Kill me," Ryder says. No one says anything; everyone stares motionless. Behind my head, in the distance I hear low gurglings, a lot of it.

"Guys, you hear that?" I ask. Everyone turns their eyes towards me "I guess not. Listen," I say. I see everyone almost feels like it got quieter.

"Oh my god," Frank says and points behind the house. We all run to the right and left side of the house, and what we saw made the color drain from everyone's faces: the herd had followed us, and it had gotten bigger, a hell of a lot bigger.

"We gotta move. Now," Claire says. The teens, including all the guards, take off running in the opposite direction of the herd, leaving Destiny, Claire, Ryder, Frank, and my group left. "Come to the house; we all are going to need weapons," Claire motions, and all of us make a break for the house. We make it to the house. They all bust into their rooms and come out with pistols, revolvers, and shotguns. Once we all have a weapon *even Jake has a pistol* and extra ammo, we peek through the windows. "We gotta come up with a plan. We don't move soon, they're going to block us in here," Claire warns.

Ryder starts coughing again, and this time almost loses his balance. Frank grabs him and sits him down on a chair. "Not to mention we have someone here that if we don't take care of now, it won't matter about the herd out there," Miko chimes in.

"I'm...I'm fine. Just leave...leave me." Ryder breathes out; he's dripping sweat, shaky, and the veins all the way to his neck are purple; the infection is spreading fast.

"I'm not leaving you," Destiny says firmly. "You guys go out through the back, I'll fend off the house as long as I can," she says.

"Destiny... no," Claire, says but Destiny shakes her head.

DESTINY'S POV

"Destiny...no" Claire tries to protest, but I shake my head. I've made up my mind. Miranda tugs on Claire's arm, and they all run out the back.

"Why..." is all Ryder can make out to ask me. I turn and pull up a chair, sitting across from him, and a few feet back.

"I don't know, I guess I owed you one." I laugh. Ryder cracks a sloppy grin. "If you would have left me in that herd when I first met you, I would have died. I can't leave you here to die like that either." I hear zombies start to bang on the windows. I jump up so fast my chair knocks over. "Ryder?" I look over at him, but he's passed out "Ryder!" I yell a little louder but still nothing. "Damn it," I say to myself. Before I can think of a plan, the window breaks and zombies start falling in the house. I quickly place my revolver in my back pocket and pick up Ryder's shotgun. *Bang* *Bang* The more I shoot, the more they come. I run to my bedroom. They haven't gotten to this side of the house, yet outside, none are by my window. I let off three more shots and close the door behind me, throwing my dresser in front of the door. If I can make it out the window, I know there's a drainpipe I could probably climb to make my way to the roof. Maybe up there I can wait for the herd to pass. Quickly opening my window, I jump out and try to land as quietly as possible. I sneak my way to the corner and start shimmying up the pipe. "This. Is. Definitely. Harder. Than what movies make it seem." I breathe heavy as my biceps and finger grip tense and ache with each pull up to the roof. I make it to the top of the house, realizing now that I am trapped, but weighing out my options, it feels best to just stay here and hope the herd passes sooner rather than later. I just sit down and stare at what looks like hundreds of zombies walking past/to my direction as the sun sets.

No food… No water… Just a few rounds for two guns… I think I know the odds of tonight. I take the deepest breath I've ever taken. "Guys," I whisper. I know no one can hear me, but if they can, someone feel it. "Please, just look out for each other. I'll be okay…" I lie down and stare up at the sky as I see the colors in it changing from an orange to blue, and I close my eyes, trying to drift to sleep.

…This seems okay…

MIKO'S POV

"Everyone, pair up! Meet at the old house!" I hear Miranda yell behind me. I can barely see anything. My chest is tightening from breathing hard. I feel someone grab my hand and make a sharp left. I don't look at who grabbed my hand; it feels like a guy's hand is all I know, but right now I don't have time to question who I'm with, I just have to stay alive. I can see our shed by the river in the distance. We must have made a wrong turn somewhere. "Too many of them to run to the house right now. We'll hide in this shed." Okay, I'm definitely not with Alex, but that doesn't sound like Daniel either. I see Jake. *Holy shit. I didn't even know he was with us,* me and, *ohhhh him.* Frank run into the shed. Frank quickly pushes a desk that is close by in front of the door to barricade it.

"So what do we do now? Now all you did was trap us in here while our friends are out there running for their lives. Why the hell wouldn't you listen to Miranda!?" I ask. We are in the middle of the house and the school; we didn't have to run much further, but I doubt he knows that.

"Thanks, Frank, for saving my ass," Frank says sarcastically, and I roll my eyes. "Anyway, I didn't know where to run, and I have no idea where we are, so I know the kid was with us. I saw shelter, so I took it," he explains.

"Ugh." I sigh in frustration. "You're right but we need to leave ASAP. We don't even have food," I say.

"I want to go save Daniel!" Jake chimes in.

"We can't right now, bud. I'm sure—" Frank gets cut off by Jake kicking him in the knee. I stifle my laugh; looks like training is paying off.

"I said now," Jake demands.

"I say if the kid wants to go out there, let him go." I shrug. Frank glares at me and turns back to Jake.

"You're not leaving. Look, Miko, we barely know each other, but we are stuck here at least until morning, so we might as well make the most of it," he tries to reason. I just nod as he starts walking around touching things. "Whoever had this place must have used it for fishing." He touched one of the fishing rods.

"Yeah…" I trail off.

"Should we tell him?" Jake whispers to me. I shake my head quickly ."Why not, he's our friend," he says.

"What?" Frank turns around.

"Nothing," I say.

"No, Miko's lying. This place—" Jake starts talking. I grab my knife and hold it to Jake's throat; he freezes in horror.

"I said no," I say to Jake coldly.

Frank looks stunned. "Miko, come on, he's just a kid. I don't even really want to know what he's saying anyway." Frank laughs. I lower my knife slowly.

"You're just as evil as Robert was," Jake says to me. My jaw drops and eyes darken. How could he say that to me? I'm nothing like that fucking monster! I don't hurt people for fun…or do I? The last few months, the world we've been trapped in, maybe it's just getting to me. I hurt people I care about, I know that, but never…no. I am like him, and not the world going to shit that made me this. I've been this way since him. I've just been getting worse every day. It's the world turning to this is what made my true self come out and that scary. I knew I could have gone either way, but I tried so hard not to be this way, to not be like this man in ANY way, but I'm a monster…. Maybe it's time I accept that.

Frank looks very confused. "You know what, Jake? I am a monster." I laugh, grabbing Jake's arm and pulling him to the door.

Jake squirms to try and break free, but I twist my fist in his shirt fabric for better grip with one hand and start pushing the desk from the door with my other. Frank quickly jumps to the door. "What the hell are you doing!?" he yells. Now that there isn't anything but Frank blocking the door, we start hearing banging and the creaking of the door trying to open. Frank quickly throws his whole body on the door, shutting it. "Miko… help!" He struggles against the door.

Without thinking, I push Frank out the way, open the door just enough, and push Jake out "Noo! I'm sorry! Nononono please…" Jake chokes out with tears streaming down his face as I push him out completely, slamming the door and sliding the table back. I pull out my knife to Frank, who tries to move the crate. We hear Jake banging on the door. "help! Help me! They gonna get me!" We hear one last high-pitch crying scream and the rising sound of gurgling coming together.

"How…how could you do that?" Frank says, without moving or even looking at me.

"You don't know what I've been through. Don't question my actions if you don't know me," I tell Frank. I try to walk away, but Frank grabs my bicep, yanking me back to him.

"If that's the case then you can go out there too," he says, opening the door. Jake's semi-eaten body lays right in front of the door, and at least eighteen zombies in front as well. "Have fun," Frank says and tries to push me out. As he pushes me, I quickly grab his wrist with my other hand, pulling myself back up and him forward. I stumble but am able to keep my balance. Frank trips over Jake's corpse. "Miko, you gotta help me!" Frank says.

I go to help Frank, but as I get closer, I feel a pull on my leg. Looking down I see a zombie on my foot. I try yanking it off, but every time I yank, it pulls. "I'm stuck!" I yell. I look over at Frank who is wrestling with zombies, falling in. I try to reach for my gun on the table; it's just out of reach.

…We're stuck; this isn't okay…

ALEX'S POV

Daniel and I make it all the way to the safe house, running inside and barricading the door. We do a quick search of the house, but it looks like no one else has gotten here yet. "They should all be here by now! What if something happened, Alex!?" Daniel yells, freaking out.

"Man, you have to calm down. There is nothing we can do now with a herd outside passing us. All we can do is wait it out," I try to reason with him, but he keeps pacing back and forth. "I know your worried about your brother," I tell him. He finally stops and looks up at me.

"It was the hardest decision I ever made letting him stay with you guys, but I thought I'd be on my own, with no food, water, or help for him. After getting with this group…they had so many ideas of building a city, starting over, being a young society. I thought I could go back to you guys and convince you to come. Or at least give me Jake back, then when I saw Miranda and Miko captured but then start to get comfortable, I thought there was hope, but now that's all gone." He sighs heavily "I guess that was on me for still having hope." Wow, I almost feel bad for this guy.

"Hey, look, man." I pause for him to look at me. "I've been taking care of Jake just as much if not more than Miranda, and I just wanted to tell you I get it. I never had siblings, so I never understood the family love you just automatically feel, well until, until I met the group. Sure, it wasn't all love and fun at first, but it had been so long…I almost forgot what family was like. Now I don't know how to live without them," I say. My eyes go wide for a brief second, realizing I actually said all that.

Daniel cracks a small smile. He looks around the house and sighs. "I just want them to be okay…. This house…gives bad vibes," he says.

"Isn't this the house that…?" Daniel nods without me needing to finish and walks off. Things must be really eating at him again seeing Jake. I hope everyone is okay and no one does anything stupid. All the gunfire, blood splattering, and zombies walking through, I couldn't see anyone. I only focused on myself. I should have helped someone, I should have called out or grabbed Miko or Jake. I'm too selfish. I sit on the steps and put my head in my hands; each second my heart beats faster.

Daniel comes up to me a few moments later. "We can't just stay around, we have to look for them," he says.

"We have to stick to the plan," I tell him, and he sighs.

"You can stay, I'm going back." Daniel pulls out his gun, and without another word, he runs out.

"Daniel!" I yell, but the door slams behind. "For fuck's sake! Daniel!" I pull out my revolver and run out after Daniel into the herd's direction.

…We better make it out okay…

ALLISON'S POV

I'm alone hiding in this sticky, damp, dark-looking cave that doesn't go that far in. As I sit along the edge of the rock wall, my heart is pounding out of my chest and my breath quickens with each inhale. I'm not far off the house, but there are a lot of zombies walking where I need to run through. I hear running footsteps, and I grab my gun and hold it to my chest. The girl who helped Miranda with her face ran in front of the "cave" entrance. "Uhh...Allison, right?" she asks as she quickly ducks in and sits across from me.

"Yeah, who are you again?" I ask, lowering my gun to my side.

"My name's Claire." She sighs and takes a look outside "I really don't want to be here. Do you have a plan?" she asks me, and I shake my head. "Ugh, how could I let this happen?" she says and bangs her head lightly back.

"What do you mean? You couldn't control this," I try to explain.

"It's not that." She shakes her head. "I know I couldn't have controlled the herd. I mean how could I let my group crumble...? I know I could have done more to keep us together and now look. We don't have a clue if any one of the last few people we care about are okay; that has to bother you as much as I do," she explains. I like her thinking, bet she's one of the reasons they wanted to stay....

"You're right, it is killing me not knowing if Miko or Miranda or Alex or anyone is okay. But we can't do anything right now but wait it out and hope everyone is okay," I try to reason.

"I don't understand how you think, Allison, but I can't think like you," she scoffs and hangs her head in between her knees.

"I think this way because if I don't I would kill myself," I say coldly. She snaps her head back up. "I couldn't live with losing any more loved ones. I would die if any of them where gone," I explain.

She doesn't say anything at first; instead, she just looks at me, processing what I just said. Then she looks at the gun I have sitting on my side. "Maybe we should," she says, pulling out her pistol. "I don't have a good feeling that Destiny made it, Ryder is already dead, Daniel wasn't who he said. Everyone. Everything I loved. It's gone or was a lie. What do I have to live for?" Tears start slowly streaming down her face, one by one.

I pick up my revolver and look back up to her. "Even if my friends are still alive, they don't need me. All I do is hold them back. They are happier on their own." I choke out a sarcastic laugh as tears start swelling in my eyes.

"On the count of three," Claire says, slowly putting the gun under her chin, closing her eyes and taking a deep breath. I close my eyes and do the same. Seeing nothing but darkness before I go seems almost peaceful; there is no one here to be hurt by seeing me suffer, no one I can see hurt, and no more stress, no more running. I'll finally get to relax and just dream about everything I could every wish for. "Ready?" she asks.

"Ready," I say.

"One," she starts.

"T-two," I continue

"Three."

Bang. *One loud bang goes off; birds scatter off the trees in a yard's radius. …I'm now okay…?*

MIRANDA'S POV

I'm running in between trees. I know I told everyone to go to the house, but when I saw the house in the distance from where I was running, it looked like it had been swarmed. I would have ran that way to see if anyone was there, but I ran out of ammo a half a mile back. I just hope no one got there before that to get trapped, and they all made the decision I did. Seeing the watch post through the distance, I got hopeful, but then I got the worst cramp and a zinging sensation down my leg, and I fall face first to the ground. "Ow, shit." I turn and sit up, holding my knee. My leg feels like it was shattered all over again; must have been too much running. Looking around, I decide to scoot back and lean my back against a tree. Rest for a few, then I'll walk as fast as I can. Once I'm there I'll have time to make a plan if no one, or not everyone is there.

After a few minutes I stand, winching slightly, and start limping back in my direction. As I'm walking behind me, I hear loud gurgling, turning around to be faced with a zombie right behind me. I jump back and end up tripping, the zombie landing on top of me. One of my hands shoots up to its forehead, the other to its chest, and I try pushing it off as its grips my shoulders trying to find any part of me to bite. "Get…off…ugh." I struggle. My heart starts beating faster as my muscles start to ache from holding it up. I can hear more coming in the distance, and my breath quickens. This isn't how I wanted to go, I wanted to die from getting sick, or killing myself even. I don't want to die from the hands of these things; they took everything from me already. All of a sudden, I hear gunshots, half the zombies forehead that was on top of me gets blown off, the blood splattering all over my face, and I quickly push it to the side and stand up with my hands up. I don't know who shot, so I have to be careful. I look around and spot one of Ryder's shooters aiming his rifle at me. "Thank—" I'm cut off by him letting of a gunshot that grazes over my left shoulder, shooting another zombie behind me.

"You. You and your people destroyed everything! You ruined my family, you took away the last place I had called home, you deserve everything that is coming your way," the guy says through gritted teeth. Before I have time to react, he shoots me in the stomach and takes off running into the woods.

I gasp for air, my hands tightly pressing over the wound. I drop to my knees "I…I can't…can't…" I choke up and spit out blood. I sit down and have my back up against another tree; saliva mixed with blood drips out the corner of my mouth. I try to steady and calm my breathing. I can feel my eyes burning with tears, and my fingers slowly getting soaked in blood through my shirt as the blood comes out faster; droplets start to run down my fingers and drip onto the floor. My whole insides feel like they are burning up, and sweat starts dripping off my forehead. My eyes slowly start to close, and I can feel my muscles start giving out no matter how hard I'm trying to keep the pressure on.

In the distance I hear, "Miranda! Miranda!" and loud running footsteps. Opening my eyes, everything I see is blurry and spinning. I can't make out anything. I try to yell but cough up more blood, and my throat starts to feel like it's closing. "Miranda!" The voice and footsteps I can hear getting closer. I can't hear the voice well enough to know who it is. In a second after that, I see a big flash of light before my body gives out completely, dropping to the side, and everything goes black.

…This wasn't supposed to happen; we were all supposed to be okay…